WHAT IF History of Australia

GOLD RUSH

Going Gold Crazy!

www.bigskypublishing.com.au

By Craig Cormick Illustrated by Cheri Hughes

First published 2022

Big Sky Publishing Pty Ltd

PO Box 303, Newport, NSW 2106, Australia

Phone: 1300 364 611
Fax: (61 2) 8330 9211

Email: info@bigskypublishing.com.au

Web: www.bigskypublishing.com.au

Cover Design and Typesetting: Cheri Hughes

Printed and bound in Australia by Griffin Press

Author: Craig Cormick

Title: What If History of Australia Gold Rush

ISBN: 9-781922-615824 (paperback)

Subjects: Middle Grade Fiction.

A catalogue record for this book is available from the National Library of Australia

WHAT IF History of Australia

GOLD RUSH

Going Gold Crazy!

By Craig Cormick Illustrated by Cheri Hughes

CONTENTS

1. Gold! Gold! Gold!....7

2. New New France – The Origin Story....20

3. Who Said Tax?....29

4. What Are the Neighbours Thinking?....34

5. Be Careful What You Wish For....39

6. To Tax or Not to Tax?....51

7. A Grand Idea....59

8. Life on the Diggings....66

9. T - A - X Spells Licence Fee....72

10. El Dorado....78

11. Let's Not Forget the Dutch....86

12. Chinese....90

13. Dealing With the Chinese Question....104

14. Planning to Invade....109

15. An Australian Civil War....113

16. The Frequently Fairly Ferocious and Fantastically Formidable French Forces....123

17. The Perfectly Pompous and Practically Pathetic British Plans....127

18. Reaching the Border River 132
19. Another Grand Idea 142
20. Eureka! 152
21. Breaking a Few Eggs 170
22. The Second Battle for Eureka 174
23. The Almost Second Battle for Eureka 177
24. Meanwhile, in New New Scotland 186
25. Having a Tough Talk About Finances 190
26. El Gladstono 195
27. Gold, Guano and Grapes 199
28. It all Comes Back to Taxes 203
29. Time to Talk about Bushrangers 207
30. Tracking the Bushrangers 230
31. Enter Ned Kelly 236
32. Nearing the End of the Century 248
33. About the Author 260

CHAPTER 1

Gold! Gold! Gold!

Have you ever looked at moment in history and asked yourself, What If it hadn't turned out that way? What if something small had changed that made a huge impact on what happened in history? Like What if the First Fleet was sent to Madagascar instead of Botany Bay? Or What if Napoleon Bonaparte had decided to take up a career as a chicken farmer?

Well then life today would have been very, very different, right?

So let's look at some of the key moments in Australian history and imagine what might have happened had just a few things been different. And I want us to look at one of the biggest impacts on Australia's development – after all the initial colonising and bad times that went with it. The discovery of gold!

Now you really only need to know one thing about gold. Not it's chemical symbol, nor how well it conducts electricity, nor even how much it weighs. The thing you need to know is that it makes people go really, really crazy.

Gold Fever, they call it. And it means you lose all your common sense and start acting like a complete idiot. I know there might be a few people in your family who you are now saying to yourself, 'Well that explains everything – they have gold fever!'

But no, there are actually a few people in everyone's family who just lack common sense and act like complete idiots regardless.

The Gold Fever we're talking about makes ordinary people act like complete crazy people only when gold is involved. And we'll have plenty of examples of that in this book.

This craziness makes some people trek up into the coldest mountains of Alaska and Canada in winter looking for specs of gold. It makes others travel up into the dry hot interior of Cape York in summer. Or it sends people deep into the central American jungles, fighting off fever and snakes, looking for an imagined city of gold.

In 1848 gold had been discovered in California in the USA – and people went crazy. Many, many thousands of people left their jobs and families and headed there from all corners of the world. (Which begs the question, why do we say 'corners of the world'? The World is round and surely doesn't have any corners?). Anyway, this was triggered by a single piece of gold about the size of a cornflake.

Try it at home some time. Get a cornflake from the pantry and hold it up in the air and say, 'I've found gold!' Before you know it there will be hundreds of people in your back yard digging everything up. (Very helpful if your toilet is blocked and your dad says the plumber wants to charge too much to dig up the pipes!).

Gold Facts and figures

- Gold is extremely ductile. A single ounce of gold can be stretched into a gold thread 8 kilometres long.
- The first gold coins were produced around 700 BC.
- Gold has been discovered on every continent on Earth.
- Gold has been mined for over 5,000 years.
- Gold is the most non-reactive of all metals and does not rust.
- Scientists in Australia have found gold particles in the leaves of Eucalyptus Trees.
- The largest gold nugget still in existence is named the "Hand of Faith" – and was found in Australia in 1980. It weighs about 27 kilograms and is currently on display at the Golden Nugget Casino in Las Vegas.
- While Nobel Prize medals are made of pure gold, modern Olympic gold medals are made of silver and then plated with a thin layer of gold.

But back to the main story. Putting on our Really Truly Historically Factual hat gold was officially found in Australia two years later, in 1851 – but I'll let you in on a secret. It had actually been found many decades earlier, by several different people. But none of them were able to trigger enough interest to get gold fever going.

As much as ten years earlier, in 1841, the Reverend William Branwhite Clarke found traces of gold in the

Blue Mountains. He knew what it was too as he was one of the earliest geologists working in the colony. He reportedly showed a sample of the gold to the Governor at the time, Sir George Gipps, who said to him, "Put it away Mr Clarke or we shall all have our throats cut." Gipps feared that the many convicts in the colony would go mad with gold fever and rebel to get at the gold.

Governor Gipps

Gold was not "officially" found in New South Wales until 1851, when Edward Hargraves found traces of gold between the towns of Orange and Bathurst. The new Governor at that time, Sir Charles Augustus FitzRoy, had offered a £10,000 reward for the discovery of gold in the colony. He was clearly not as afraid of gold fever as Governor Gipps had been.

And Edward Hargraves had recently returned from California where he had failed to find gold, but had found that the land there looked rather similar to parts of New South Wales. And that got him thinking.

Or to put it very simply, Governor FitzRoy wanted someone to find gold and help make the colony rich and Edward Hargraves wanted someone to throw money at him for doing the least amount of work possible. A perfect match, yes?

Governor FitzRoy

Now let's put on our What If history hat and look at how history might have turned out differently if Edward Hargraves had found gold in California, and never came back to New South Wales. What if he became a lazy conman over there instead of here, and nobody had "officially" found gold in New South Scotland for some time still? (Quick reminder: The French had settled where modern Melbourne is and called their colony New New France – so as not to be confused with New France in North America – and the British had settled around Port Jackson and called their colony New South Scotland. Clear?).

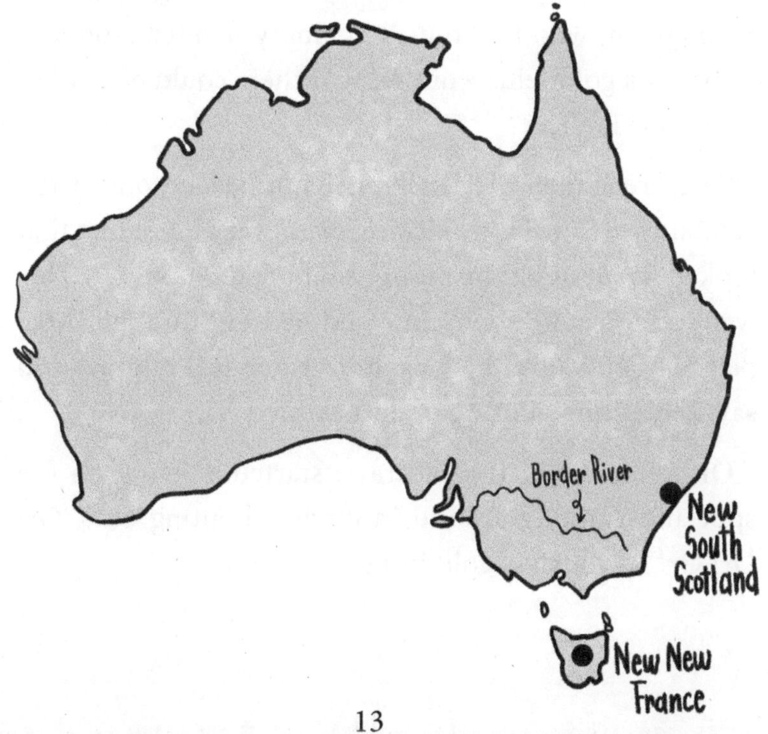

What if in this What If version of history, gold was first discovered in New New France by the French? How different might things have been then?

So here's the scene: We have the British and French settlements divided by the Border River – and while neither much liked the other they knew that a war between them would be ridiculously expensive and no one in their right mind would want to do that.

Unless of course gold had been discovered in one of the colonies and not in the other. Then people would lose their common sense and make some crazy decisions.

And in our What If history we have got several Frenchmen, who had returned empty-handed from the California goldfields wondering if there could be gold in New New France?

One Frenchman, Henri Frencham, headed out of the capital city, New Paris, kicking over every bit of dirt that looked like it might be hiding a bit of gold under it. This went on for quite some time and he went through three pairs of boots until he kicked over one tuft of grass and saw something glinting underneath.

Or course he just went crazy, started dancing on the spot and running around in circles shouting out, "Or! Or! Or!" – which is gold in French.

Or.
Or.
Or.
Or what?

He rushed back to the city with the sample of gold he had found and waited to be become rich and famous. But the city officials examined the rock he had brought in and said it was not actually gold. Here's a sad fact – there are rocks that can easily be mistaken for gold. You might have heard the name fool's gold. Or in French *l'or des fous!* (Try and remember that, you never know when it might come in useful!).

There was no dancing and running in circles after that, and Henri Frencham still had to go and buy a new pair of boots.

But about the same time a group of friends had the same idea as Henri and went looking for gold northeast of New Paris. They had a more advanced method than just kicking over tufts of grass and actually dug up the ground. And they found gold in large quantities and the colonial government granted them the first gold mining licence.

Then the newspapers of the day went crazy. As did the citizens of New New France. Hundreds rushed to the area, and in other parts of the colony every man, woman and child with a shovel started digging up their backyards in the hope of striking it rich. And some did, particularly near the towns of Le Ballarat and Le Bendigo.

Of interest, the First Nations people of New New France had known about the existence of gold for a long, long time. Even if they could not understand the French craziness for this metal that was too soft to make tools out of – they knew where to find it. If only somebody had just asked them.

But nobody did. So once again the European settlers were proudly proclaiming they had discovered something that had long been known to exist by the locals.

Edward Hargraves

Edward Hargraves was a man who liked to write his own history. Unfortunately it didn't always align with official histories. We do know that he was born in England and came out to Australia as a young lad, working in a variety of jobs before deciding to lead a small group to the Californian goldfields in 1850.

The key lesson he learned there appears to have been that the people who got the richest let others do their work for them. So when he returned to Australia in 1851 he went looking for people who said they had already found traces of gold.

He found several such men near Bathurst, and he formed a partnership with John Lister, and two brothers, William Tom and James Tom. They took him to Lewis Ponds Creek where they had previously found small amounts of gold.

In his own history, which doesn't really mention his partners, he said, "At that instant, I felt myself to be a great man". He also said that he would become a baronet and his horse would be stuffed, put in a glass case and sent to the British Museum.

He hurried back to Sydney to proclaim he had found gold, and wanted to claim the £10,000 pound reward that the colony had put up for its discovery. Interestingly, the main reason for the reward was to try and stop the large numbers of people leaving the colony and going to California.

But Hargraves was told his flecks were not large enough to count as a discovery. Bitterly disappointed he went back to Bathurst and found his partners had meanwhile discovered much more gold. So what did he do? Take them with him to Sydney and proclaim they had all discovered more gold? Of course not, he took it back to Sydney by himself and claimed the reward for himself!

When he had proclaimed that he felt himself a great man – he clearly meant a great conman and a great ratbag.

He also told everybody he could about the discovery, despite his 'partners' asking him to keep it a secret.

So the word was out – a gold rush had started – and Hargraves became as famous as he predicted and even got to meet Queen Victoria. However his horse did not get stuffed and put in the British Museum!

CHAPTER 2

New New France – The Origin Story

Time to tell the origin story of New New France, I think. Book one in this series told how Captain Cook's ship sunk when it hit the Great Barrier Reef in 1770 and he never got back to England with his charts and instead the East Coast of Australia was charted by the Frenchman La Perouse. And instead of his ships sinking when they hit a reef he got back to France and told everyone what he had found and the French decided to set up a colony there. New New Paris, on the shores of Port Philippe Bay!

Then when the French Revolution broke out in 1789 French royalists fled to settle the colony. And soon the King, Louis 16th, escaped and joined them. Things were going well until Napoleon was deposed by a coalition of European countries in 1814 and exiled to the colony too.

Things got a bit tense with the two rulers trying to out-rule each other – but settled down after they had both died in 1825 and the King's son, Louis 17th proposed marriage to Napoleon's widow, Marie-Louise. He was 40 and she was 34, and they had time enough to pop out a kid before they felt like retiring or passing away in the late 1840s.

Their son became Louis 19th or Napoleon 2.5. (This was because Napoleon already had a son, born in 1811 who wanted to use the title Napoleon 2nd, and his cousin was going to be made ruler of France in 1852 and be known as Napoleon 3rd).

Keeping up? If not, you only need to know that by 1850 there was a 22-year-old ruler on the throne of New New France, and the colony was a democratic monarchy, where you could both vote for your leader and also have a king rule over you at the same time. It was confusing to many, but the colonists sort of got used to it.

Sort of.

Anyway, a little bit more news from the other side of the world, putting our Really Truly Historically Factual hat back on for a short bit. In the late 1840s, just before gold was discovered, there had been political turmoil all over the place.

Canada had taken peaceful steps towards becoming independent from Britain, Ireland tried hard for self-government too but was denied it, which led to violence. And not having recovered from the terrible potato famine of 1845-47, many Irish people were deciding to emigrate somewhere better. There were also riots for freedom in many other countries of Europe, and in the USA there was growing tensions over the issue of slavery with the southern states lining up for a fight with the northern states.

In China the Tai Ping rebellion against the Manchu rulers was also just getting underway.

And in France popular riots led to the then King, 75-year-old Louis-Philippe I, abdicating in 1848 in favour of his ten-year-old grandson, Louis-Philippe II. Now one thing history teaches us is that if you are going to hand power over to a 10-year-old child, you'd better be standing far, far away.

CHAPTER 2

And that's just what Louis-Philippe did. He jumped on a boat and put as much distance between himself and France as was possible And where do you go to when you have been deposed as leader of France? Well – you could go to lots and lots of countries if you had enough money, but when it started to run out you'd probably end up in New New France.

Another thing that history teaches us is that when a colony starts getting a stable form of government, the two things the ruler does not want to wake up and hear about is: 1) a rival ruler has arrived unannounced and wants to run the place, and 2) gold has been discovered and everyone is acting like complete idiots.

Imagine the scene, Louis 19/Napoleon 2.5 is having a sleep in and thinking how he might spend the day… when an aide walks in and makes that low coughing sound people make when they want to get your attention without actually using any words to get your attention.

'Oui?' ask Louis-Napoleon. 'Do you have a cough?'

'Non,' says the aide. 'It is that thing you do when you want to catch someone's attention.'

'Like this?' asks Louis-Napoleon, waving his hands around in the air. 'Hey you!'

'I will try than next time,' says the aide. 'Perhaps.'

‘Very good,’ says Louis-Napoleon. ‘Is there anything else?’

‘Well yes, your highness,’ says the aide.

‘You address me wrongly. It is a Tuesday, non? On Tuesdays I am your excellency, as I am Emperor. Tomorrow I will be your highness again, when I am King.’

‘It is Wednesday your… your highness.’

‘Oh, then I had better put on my Kingly robe, not this Emperor one.’

‘Yes, your majesty.’

‘Is there something else you wish to tell me, other than it being Wednesday.’

‘Well, yes your majesty. Some unexpected news has arrived.’

‘Oh no, I hate surprises. More turmoil in France?’

‘Well, yes, but this turmoil is closer to home.’

‘What is it?’

‘Gold.’

‘Gold what?’

‘Gold has been discovered, your majesty. Not too far from the city.’

‘Well, that is good news, yes? We shall all be rich.’

'Um, not necessarily your majesty.'

'Of course we will. Fetch my Minister for the Treasury. We have plans to make.'

'He has resigned and gone to dig for gold.'

'What? The unfaithful dog! Then fetch me my Minister for anything else.'

'They have all resigned and gone to dig for gold.'

'How dare they! This is most upsetting. Call for the cook, I feel like something soothing for breakfast.'

'Uh, all the cooks have left too.'

'What? Well, that is very serious. Very, very serious. Is that the second news you had to tell me?'

'No, your majesty. Something else.'

'Go on then.'

'We have an unexpected visitor from France.'

'Splendid. It has been a long time since we had a visitor.'

'Perhaps not so splendid.'

'Are you are trying to tell me that this is not a good visitor?'

'Well, your majesty, let me just say, perhaps it is not.'

'Oh, no! It's not King Louis-Philippe is it? He hasn't been thrown out of office, has he?'

'Yes, I am afraid that is the case.'

Louis-Napoleon sighs heavily. 'And I suppose he'll want to try and rule things here.'

'I expect he will.'

'Well, we'll have to put a stop to it. I'm a monarch every second day, after all. Though maybe I should make him wait until tomorrow so I can confront him as Emperor rather than as King?'

'A splendid idea, your majesty.'

'Yes, we'll do that. Have the senior aide make up a room for him in one of the cottages near the sewage farm.'

'I am afraid the senior aide has left to go and dig for gold too.'

'So who is left?'

'Well, there's me, your majesty. But I have a letter here for you.'

'Oh? Who is it from?'

'It is from me. It is my letter of resignation. Adieu your majesty. I'm going to dig for gold too.'

(Editor's note: Several French swear words removed from the book here!).

CHAPTER 3

Who Said Tax?

So here we are with the population of New Paris quitting their jobs and heading off into the countryside to dig for gold, and all the ships sitting in the harbour with no crew and the shops with no people to work in them and the nobles with no servants.

What would you do if you were in charge?

Well, after consulting with his new Ministers, Louis-Napoleon decides to open up the colony to immigration, hoping to fill all those empty jobs. That sounds a fair plan. But did that happen?

Well, no, of course not. I mean you did have lots of Irish and Chinese and others who were more than happy to move to a new land, as things weren't looking very happy in their own countries. But gold, remember. Losing all common sense, remember. Completely idiotic, remember.

Yes, all those thousands of people who moved to New New France weren't really interested in working on the ships, or in the shops or in the fancy homes. They just wanted to get a shovel and bucket and head to the gold diggings and get rich quickly.

Now here's another lesson from history that you can apply to many situations in life: things that look too good to be true, generally aren't true. And that applies particularly to any get-rich-quick schemes. Trust me on this! Whether it's a scammer phone call or email, or even the belief that writing a kid's book will make you rich enough to sit by the pool all day in the sunshine. It always sounds tempting and easy to believe – but the closest you actually get to that is a rickety chair by an old bucket in the backyard full of rainwater. Um, sorry, maybe I'm getting off the track a bit, but you get the point, yes?

Anyway, back in the 1850s they didn't have scammer phone calls or emails trying to trick you into giving them your bank account details – but they did have lots of people like Edward Hargraves, promising you that you would become rich quickly if you only followed their advice.

And a very few did get rich. Very rich. And they had jewellery and clothing ornaments made from gold to show everyone how rich they were. One guy even gave his horse gold horseshoes!

But while there were tens of thousands of migrants now digging up much of the land looking for gold – the people who were really getting rich were those who were selling them over-priced food and equipment. Or selling shares in mining companies. Or even selling maps and mine leases, that weren't worth very much.

None of this was making Louis-Napoleon any happier, with hordes of non-French-speaking people all over the colony, digging it up like a plague of wombats, and none of the money moving into the King/Emperor's coffers.

But things changed when he started complaining to King Louis-Philippe about it one day, having become frenemies of sorts. In the months that had passed since his arrival Louis-Napoleon decided he wasn't too bad for an old, deposed ruler, who didn't know how to dab, and didn't know any of the cool new words that younger people like him used. He often invited him around for tea, on those days he was a king and not an emperor.

And on this day, as he complained about the influx of migrants who were changing the colony in ways he did not like, Louis-Philippe said, 'Why aren't you taxing the miners?'

And it was like a light bulb went on over Louis-Napoleon's head. (Except that light bulbs had not been invented yet. So maybe it was more like a really, really bright candle ignited over his head.) 'Of course,' he said. 'I just need to tax the people more and everything will be alright.'

Yeah, like that has always worked out well in history! And like miners in Australia have ever put up with anyone suggesting they pay a fair share of tax on what they dig up!

Things were now on a course to get ugly. But we'll get to that by and by. First, we need to look at what was happening over the borders – in New South Scotland, Nuevo Nuevo Spain and New New Holland.

CHAPTER 4

What Are the Neighbours Thinking?

In our What If version of history the territory that is now Queensland had been settled by the Spanish, with the city of Nuevo Neuvo Madrid roughly where Brisbane is. Unlike Spain's colonies in South America, the colony here had not taken part in the great struggles for independence from Spain they fought in the 1820s.

The main difference was that the South American colonies had many, many locally-born people, and were relatively rich. And history shows us that when you have a lot of locally-born people who are relatively rich, but are sending their riches back to the colonising country – they soon get sick of it and want to keep their wealth. (Think of the colonies of North America and the War of Independence from Britain as an example).

After a series of battles and struggles the countries of South America one by one declared their independence from Spain. In Nuevo Nuevo Spain, however, the colony's economy was largely paid for by Spain, and they had no desire to become independent, as they knew it would take them from being a poor Spanish colony to becoming an even poorer one.

Unless, perhaps, gold might be discovered. That would change everything, wouldn't it?

***

And over in New New Holland, roughly where South Australia is now, the Dutch colonial powers were thinking along similar lines. They had built their settlement where it was because all their maps told them that Western Australia had too much desert and too many flies. So, they found a nice spot in South Australia and started acting all snooty to the British about not having any convicts there, and started acting snooty to the French about all the theatres and canals they had built.

Anyway, like the colonists in Nuevo Nuevo Spain, they were quite happy to have the Dutch Government pay their bills. But if they suddenly became rich, they would be willing to change that attitude pretty quickly.

And we probably need a little bit of background here about the Dutch East India Company, which had become the world's first multinational corporation. Established after the Dutch discovered trade routes to Southeast Asia, the Dutch East India Company soon controlled all the key trade between Asia and Europe and had established colonies in South Africa, Jakarta, and key trading posts right across Asia.

All over Asia there were things that the markets in Europe wanted – like cheap plastic toys and imitation designer handbags – no hang on, I've slipped into the wrong era. There were spices and exotic cloths like silk, and there were porcelains and – well, yeah, imitation designer handbags too. And the Dutch shipped these from Asia to the Europe and were making a fortune.

The Dutch East India Company ruled supreme for about 200 years, but then made a few mistakes that a lot of multinationals make. Firstly, it didn't pay enough attention to its rivals – in this case the English East India Company – which worked hard to do a better job of business while sinking Dutch ships. Secondly, it treated its staff terribly, paying them poorly which led to a lot of unhappiness and corruption. And thirdly, it treated its shareholders too well. In fact, it often paid them more than it was earning.

It does not take a maths whizz to figure out that paying your bosses more than you are earning, while paying your workers rubbish rates, is not a great business model. As a result, like a lot of chain stores that you might see at the local mall that suddenly disappear – the Dutch East India Company collapsed in 1800.

For the Dutch colonies this meant they had to do a lot more on their own, and had to turn to the Dutch Government for help.

To imagine what that was like, think of a young adult, just out of high school maybe, who has their own job and their own money and their own place and everything. And suddenly they lose that job and have to ask their parents for help with things – and even go back to live with them and follow their parents' rules. You get the idea, yeah?

So the Dutch in New New Amsterdam were also thinking, if only we had a new job – oops – if only we could find gold, things would all be good again.

CHAPTER 5

Be Careful What You Wish For

So pretty much all the colonies are looking at New New France and wishing they had gold as well. Or at least wishing they had a way to get the gold that New New France had. You might think that not particularly sensible thinking – but I think by now we all know that gold makes people more than a little bit crazy. And jealous.

And the most jealous of all the colonies was New South Scotland, of course. I mean the French and English had a lot of history of being jealous of each other and blaming each other for things like bad cuisine and bad manners. Also, the French had previously tried to invade New South Scotland under Napoleon, but it hadn't worked out so well.

The Governor at this time was Charles FitzRoy, who had been a solider before moving into the job of being Governor. He wanted friends more than he wanted to be a firm Governor and was often accused of making rules to keep people happy. He also had a reputation for driving his carriage too fast around town like maybe your Uncle Barry, and hanging around with the all the ladies too much (also a bit like Uncle Barry).

But he did have one of the greatest set of sideburns that you're ever likely to see, and famously said of the impact of gold on people that it was "unhinging the minds of all classes". And I can never understand why he isn't more famous just for that line alone.

CHAPTER 5

Governor FitzRoy was suffering even worse labour shortages than the French in New New Paris. Firstly, lots of people had gone to California when they heard of the gold rush there, and any who had not gone had now gone over the Border River to look for gold in New New France.

You can imagine the scene in the Governor's office, with his two top aides, each trying to advise him on a different strategy.

'We should invade New New France,' says the military aide.

'No, no. That would have grave consequences. We just need to find a way to get some of that French gold,' says the civilian aide.

'We need a fleet of buccaneers,' says the military aide. 'Like we did when we stole the gold that the Spanish had found in South America.'

'Pirates!' says the civilian aide. 'We have agreed to outlaw piracy.'

'Not pirates,' says the military aide. 'Buccaneers!'

'Is there a difference?' asks Governor FitzRoy.

'Yes,' says the military aide.

'No,' says the civilian aide.

Governor Gipps vs Governor FitzRoy

The two Governors could have hardly been more different. Governor Gipps, for example, who ruled from 1838 to 1846 was considered very strict and set in his ways and unlikely to ever change them. But Governor FitzRoy, who replaced him from 1846 to 1855 was considered more easy-going and adaptable to changes.

'If we don't find a way to get some of that gold we shall soon be both bankrupt and depopulated. As a Governor I'll be a failure. I wish we had our own gold.'

'We should invade,' says the military aide again.

'Perhaps we have gold here in this colony?' says the civilian aide. 'All we need to do is to post a reward for anyone who finds it?'

'Now there's an idea,' says the Governor.

Governor Gipps, the son of a clergyman, did not approve of drinking and almost never dined out anywhere, while Governor FitzRoy was known to enjoy drinking, and he and his wife were at all the parties and balls around.

Governor Gipps was promoted to the position of Governor because of his record of hard work, while Governor FitzRoy was an aristocrat who was given the position because of the people he knew in power in England.

Governor Gipps was not well loved by the wealthy landowners in the colonies, while Governor FitzRoy seemed to just want to be loved by them.

Governor Gipps wrote long and detailed reports to the Colonial Office on just about everything possible, while Governor FitzRoy had his aides write them and often chose to ignore directives given to him. Not really the type of guy you want in charge of a colony when things get difficult!

Then his maid, who has been pouring tea and listening to the conversation, says, 'It seems to me that you have already invaded New New France, with thousands of our people there, and we are profiting from their gold as most of it is sent back here.'

Governor FitzRoy looks at his two aides and then looks back at her. Then he realises she is right. They do not need to go to war. He also realises that he probably needs to fire his two aides and replace them with his maid.

But just when the Governor and his (m)aide thought they had everything under control the Tom brothers announced that they found gold near Bathurst. (Without any help from Edward Hargrave and his horse – who was still in California).

This created a few benefits, but also some major problems for the Governor. The first benefit was that they had their own gold now and didn't have to think of more ways to get the French gold. But they would have lots of Frenchmen rushing over the border in the expectation that the British gold would be better – of course – and taking their gold the same way that the settlers of New South Scotland were taking the French gold.

Then there would be the thousands of immigrants from the USA and Ireland and Italy and China, and just about everywhere else where people had been suffering poverty, thinking they could get rich quick. And by watching what had happened in New New France the Governor knew that it would mean crowds of rowdy, lawless men with guns, fighting over whatever gold they could find.

And there was another problem. A really big problem. The gold had been found on the land of the First Nations people.

Let me explain. In Really Truly Historically Factual history, when the Bathurst area had been settled, the locals were not too happy about it. All these whitefellahs bringing sheep and chopping down trees and pushing them off their land. And that led to a lot of violence, which lasted a long time and cost a large loss of life. And it didn't end very well for the First Nations people, I can tell you.

But what if in our What If version of history, the Wiradjuri people had been so successful in fighting off the settlers and colonial forces that the Government had decided to settle for peace. They came to an agreement that those areas of land that had not already been settled would remain Wiradjuri land. Settlers could cross the land, but not settle on it. And not ruin it with sheep and digging holes in it everywhere.

Governor FitzRoy was in a real pickle (which is quite an odd expression when you think about it). What was he to do? Perhaps he could have negotiated leasing arrangements where miners had to pay royalties to the Wiradjuri? Or perhaps they could have come to an agreement about where the miners could dig for gold and where they could not? Or perhaps they could just rip up the agreement and let the miners dig wherever they pleased?

Or all of the above?

And if you don't know already, Australia has a bit of a poor track record in too often making decisions in favour of miners, when it comes to miners vs First Nations people.

And we could say that Governor FitzRoy was likely to make the wrong decision because he was worried about several hundred thousand angry miners and what they might do. Or we could say that he was going to make the wrong decision because he just didn't really understand the Wiradjuri's relationship to their land, and why he couldn't just tell them to go and live on the land of some other people. Or we could just say he was a bit of a colonial racist.

So here's another fact from history that you need to understand – a lot of the early settlers were pretty racist and sexist and not the type of people you'd invite to a family barbeque by choice. They really did believe that they were superior to other peoples, just by being British. And that anybody who was not as technologically developed as them was inferior. They believed that if a people did not improve the land by building fences and houses, then they were not really occupying the land, and the British therefore had the right to occupy it.

There were exceptions to this of course, and there were many settlers who fought hard for the rights of First Nations people – and sometimes Colonial Governors were very sympathetic to their arguments. But in general, whenever it was a decision between First Nations people and money – the money won out.

Windradyne

Following the establishment of Bathurst in central New South Wales on Wiradjuri Country in 1815, there were increased tensions between settlers and Wiradjuri people as native food became scarcer and sacred sites were destroyed.

Windradyne, a northern Wiradjuri man, was one of the leaders of the resistance against the settlers. Known as 'Saturday' by the settlers, he was described by the Sydney Gazette as "One of the finest looking natives we have seen in this part of the country."

One of the triggers for Windradyne to take up arms typified the difference in European and First Nation's attitude to land and how it was shared. Having been given potatoes one day by a farmer, Windradyne and his family returned later to dig up some more potatoes. But the farmer was not now willing to share, and chased them off the land, killing several of the Wiradjuri people, including Windradyne's wife.

In response Windradyne led guerrilla attacks on farms and livestock in the region, killing several convict workers.

The settlers decided to retaliate and in 1824 massacred many Wiradjuri people including women and children, by tricking them to come to a peace feast and then killing them. This in turn triggered more revenge attacks.

Eventually the Governor had to declare Martial Law – the only time this was ever declared in Australia - and send in the military, with permission to shoot to kill. This forced many Wiradjuri to surrender.

But Windradyne only surrendered on his own terms. He marched all the way across the Blue Mountains into Parramatta, where the Governor was holding a feast, with the word "peace" in English on his hat.

This has been described as a brave gesture that ended the violence and saved the lives of many of his people.

But let's roll that What If dice and choose to go down another path. What if Governor FitzRoy decided to honour the arrangement with the Wiradjuri people, and rather than steal their land he made deals with them over access to the gold.

In return for letting miners onto some parts of their land they would be paid a percentage of the profits from the gold that was dug up. The Colonial Government would likely try and ensure that money was spent on building houses and schools and hospitals and roads, of course – employing the European builders and laborers.

But what if it was decided the Wiradjuri could use the money however they chose? They might buy better weapons for hunting, or they might use it to buy education for their children, or they might have signs built along the borders of their lands telling trespassers to honour the land and keep out. Or they might even use it to set up schools to teach the children of settlers about their culture.

Who knows what might happen when we roll that What If dice?

CHAPTER 6

To Tax or Not to Tax?

Now we have a situation where there is a crazy gold rush in New New France, and an emerging gold rush in New South Scotland, and of course each colony wants to be the one that gets all the gold that is being dug up.

So Louis-Napoleon's people in New New France start spreading stories that their gold is far superior to that of New South Scotland, and also that there is a lot more of it. This of course prompts Governor FitzRoy's people in New South Scotland to start spreading stories that you can't get into New New France unless you speak French fluently, but to get into New South Scotland you only need to be able to spell your own name. Or something very close to it.

In reply the French start a story that the gold in New South Scotland is really iron, painted yellow. And in reply to that the British start pushing the ultimate fear campaign – saying that miners in New New France will have to pay tax on their gold!

Did I mention that nothing makes a miner more deranged than they already are except the idea of having to pay taxes on what they dig up?

Well – that last message backfires a little as both colonies soon realise the only way they can really make a profit from all this gold is to find a way to tax it.

And as it is, the miners in New South Scotland already have to pay royalties to the First Nations people whose land they are digging up.

Clearly they have a predicament!

The meeting with the Governor FitzRoy and his top aides, trying to figure out what to do, goes something like this.

'I fear we may have been too clever altogether,' says the Governor, letting his impressive sideburns move regally as he talks.

His chief aide – his former maid – says, 'I said it wasn't a good idea to mention taxes.'

'But you support taxes,' says the military advisor, who has gotten his job back after much grovelling and begging.

'Oh yes,' she says. 'It's the only fair way to redistribute wealth. But I said you shouldn't mention taxes. Implement them, yes, but for heaven's sake don't talk about them.'

'I've an idea,' says the administrative aide, who has also gotten his job back, after unsuccessfully trying to find gold near Bathurst. 'What if we find a way to actually get some of the gold for ourselves? I mean, we could start a government-funded mining company, and dig for gold for ourselves.'

The top aide looks at him and says, 'No. That rarely works. Much better to tax the wealth of others than to speculate ourselves.'

'But we could get rich,' says the administrative aide.

'The same way you got rich at the diggings?' she asks.

There is quiet in the small room as the men look at the bookshelves and windows and ornate teacups in front of them. They all know that the administrative aide lost not only all his savings in his recent search for gold, but came back to Sydney with no shirt or trousers, dressed only in a wide-brimmed hat.

'But surely the principle is sound,' he says softly.

'Quite sound,' says the Governor, not wanting the poor fellow to be humiliated in front of the woman who used to pour his tea. After all, he is the Governor who wants everyone to like him, and this was a time when most men were pretty sexist and talked down to women. (They'd learn their lessons slowly though!).

'Tell me this then,' says the top aide. 'Is Spain a rich country or a poor country?' She looks at all the three men in turn.

'A rather poor country, I would say,' says the Governor.

'And are England and France rich countries or poor countries?' she asks.

'Oh – I know this one,' says the administrative aide. 'Rather rich countries.'

'Yes,' says the top aide. 'And can you tell me which of those three countries found thousands and thousands of pounds worth of gold in South America?'

The military aide closes his eyes a moment, as if searching for the trick in the question. Finally, he says, 'It was Spain, wasn't it?'

'Of course it was,' she says. 'But where did all that gold go to?'

The three men look around the study once more, at the bookshelves and windows and ornate teacups again, as if they might find inspiration there. But there is nothing that gives them an answer.

'I'll tell you,' she says. 'It all went to England and France.'

'Did it by Jove?' says the Governor. 'That was very clever.'

'It was all the buccaneers we had working for us, wasn't it,' says the military aide. 'Didn't I argue just that, that we should employ buccaneers, or maybe bushrangers, to steal the French gold and bring it back here?'

The top aide shakes her head a little. 'It was not due to the buccaneers. Well, a little bit of it was, but the most important thing was that England and France built industries and made things, and the Spanish bought lots and lots of those things.'

She sees the men are trying to grasp what she is saying. So she spells it out slowly and carefully. 'We make things. The Spanish buy things. They give us their gold. We develop industries. The Spanish need to keep buying things to replace what they have already bought. We keep making things. They soon have no gold, and lots of useless things that they can't sell, and we have an established industry and we have the gold.'

'Oh, I see,' says the Governor. 'That is very clever, isn't it.'

'Very, very clever,' says the administrative aide. 'Why didn't we think of that?'

The top aide decides to not tell them that if they had the brains to think of such things they would be working for the government in London, not looking after a former convict colony on the far side of the world.

'Wait a minute,' says the Governor. 'I can see a flaw in your plan.'

'Yes?' she asks.

'If we were to copy that strategy here, it would mean setting up industries and making things the French actually wanted to buy.'

'Oh dear,' says the administrative aide. 'I see your point.'

'What point?' she asks.

'It would mean doing some very hard work.' He holds up his cup of tea to his mouth, to indicate that is the only heavy lifting that he is prepared to do in a day.

The administrative aide shakes his head. 'A pity. The idea sounded like it had a lot of potential. Well, at first.'

'Wait a minute,' says the military advisor. 'Did I miss something? Where do the buccaneer bushrangers come into this?'

Gold Locations by State or Territory

In the 30 years after gold was first officially discovered at Ophir, near Bathurst in New South Wales in 1851, gold was found at over 60 sites across Australia. Some of the key locations – which might be near where you live – and the dates of discovery were:

New South Wales

- Hill End, 1851
- Tilba Tilba, 1852
- Kiandra, 1860
- Young, 1860
- Forbes, 1861
- Parkes, 1862
- Gulgong, 1870

Victoria

- Clunes, 1851
- Anderson's Creek, Warrandyte, 1851
- Castlemaine, 1851
- Buninyong, 1851
- Ballarat, 1851
- Bendigo, 1851

continued...

continued...

- Beechworth, 1852
- Yackandandah, 1852
- Eaglehawk, May 1852
- Omeo, 1852
- Heathcote, 1852
- Buckland River, 1853
- Creswick, 1853
- Ararat, 1854
- Blackwood, 1855
- Stawell, 1857
- Chiltern 1858
- Wood's Point, 1862

South Australia

- Onkaparinga, 1852
- Teetulpa, 1886
- Western Australia
- Hall's Creek, 1885
- The Pilbara, 1888
- Southern Cross, 1888
- Coolgardie, 1892
- Kalgoorlie, 1893

Queensland

- Rockhampton, 1858
- Gympie, 1867
- Charters Towers, 1872
- Palmer River, near Cooktown, 1873
- Hodgkinson River, near Cairns, 1875
- Coen, 1878
- Croydon, 1885

Northern Territory

- Pine Creek, 1871

CHAPTER 7

A Grand Idea

And of course in New New France they were having difficult conversations of their own. The influx of diggers had been larger than anybody had expected.

And whether we are wearing our What If history hat, or our Really Truly Historically Factual hat, the population was on its way to quadrupling from 430,000 people to 1.7 million over 20 years, as people from across the world arrived in search of gold.

But instead of making a lot of money Louis-Napoleon found having all these diggers was costing him a lot of money. He had to pay higher wages to people to stay and work for him, he had to pay more for food and wine since all the merchants in the city were selling everything they could to the miners, and he had to pay people to keep an eye on Louis-Philippe to make sure he was not plotting to take over the place.

Added to that was a rapid increase in lawlessness – even in the city – as most of New New Paris' police had resigned and gone to the goldfields.

Louis-Napoleon needed to find a way to raise money, but all around him were rich aristocrats who no intention of ever paying taxes. True they had all been granted large tracts of land by his grandfather Louis XVI, and they had grown very rich with sheep and cattle – but let me tell you, it was even harder to get a French landowner to pay taxes than it was to get a miner to pay taxes.

Several times his advisers had suggested he start taxing the miners, but whenever that was suggested, somebody would say, 'Non, it will lead to a revolution! Remember what happened in France when they tried to tax the miners.' And of course, Louis-Napoleon, who never found history his strongest subject, began to believe that was the actual cause of the French Revolution. (Just one example of what happens if you don't learn history!).

Things were so desperate that he even invited Louis-Philippe to tea to ask his opinion on things. The meeting went something like this.

'Do you have any cucumber sandwiches?' Louis-Philippe asks. 'I remember you had some last time.'

'There are none to be had,' says Louis-Napoleon, trying to remember the day of the week and if he is a King or and Emperor. 'The merchants have sent them all to the goldfields.'

'Nonsense,' says Louis-Philippe. 'Miners are too common for eating cucumbers.'

'Not at all,' says Louis-Napoleon. 'They not only eat cucumbers, but all the caviar and truffles have been sent to the diggings too.'

'So it is really that bad then?' asks Louis-Philippe.

'Worse,' says Louis-Napoleon.

The two men tut-tut for a while and drink tea out of very expensive teacups. Then Louis-Philippe finally says, 'I think I might have a grand idea that is the solution to your problem, you know.'

'Ah yes?' asks Louis-Napoleon, trying to pretend he isn't really interested in any idea that might make things easier for him. Particularly from an old man who doesn't know how to dab.

'It's all about getting your hands on gold, yes?'

Louis-Napoleon waves a hand dismissively. If Louis-Philippe is going to suggest he go out and dig some holes in his Royal Garden and search for gold himself, this will be his last visit to the Royal Residence.

'But the people on our diggings refuse to give any of it up,' he says.

'I never said the gold on our diggings,' says Louis-Philippe slyly.

'What do you mean?' asks Louis-Napoleon, very interested now.

'We simply need to get our hands on some of the gold being dug up in New South Scotland.'

King, or maybe Emperor, Louis-Napoleon sits back in his seat. A wide smile spreads across his face. Of course! It was so simple. He only has to get some of the gold from over the border and then he could afford to pay for more police and more servants and buy all the cucumbers, caviar and truffles in the colony.

But then the wide smile closes up tight again. 'How?' he asks.

'Aha,' says Louis-Philippe. 'That is the key question. And something I'd only consider discussing if I had a senior post in Government.'

Louis-Napoleon looks at him and frowns. The man has him in a bind. If he throws him out, he will never figure out on his own how to get the gold from New South Scotland. But if he gives Louis-Philippe a senior post in Government it will be like inviting him to overthrow him.

So instead of answering, Louis-Napoleon looks at his ornate clock and says, 'Oh my, is that the time already? I have an important meeting with my senior advisors. Let me think about your proposal and get back to you.'

He might not have learned much from history, but he had learned a lot about how to govern a colony – much of which involved never giving a straight answer to a hard question. Or knowing when to steal somebody else's grand ideas.

Who had the biggest nugget?

Well, depending on who you talk to, the biggest nugget of gold ever found in Australia was either the Welcome Stranger Gold nugget, or the Holtermann nugget.

The Welcome Stranger nugget was discovered by two miners from England, John Deason and Richard Oates, who were mining in central Victoria at a place called Bulldog Gully. (Yes, they could have called the nugget the Bulldog, or the Deason-Oates, or they could even have called it You Beauty, but they didn't!).

On 5 February 1869 they struck a single nugget that turned out to weigh about 70 kilograms. Much more than you or me. (Well, okay, much more than you not me!).

It was so large that it had to be broken apart on an anvil just to be weighed. They received almost £10,000 for the nugget – which in your and my pocket money would be worth about $4 million today.

The Holtermann nugget was found in 1872 in Hill End, New South Wales. It was not strictly speaking found by the German miner Bernhardt Otto Holtermann, and it was not strictly speaking a nugget – as it was gold mixed in with rock. But he was photographed standing next to it – a large slab almost as big as himself. And we all know that if you photograph something and post it on social media (well, the equivalent of social media in 1872!) then that makes it true.

The gold in the rock was estimated to be worth £12,000 – so more than the Welcome Stranger in total – and worth even more than $4 million in today's pocket money.

CHAPTER 8

Life on the Diggings

So everyone was now losing their common senses and spending all their efforts worrying about how they could get more gold. The governor of New South Scotland was becoming obsessed with getting more of the French gold. And King-Emperor Louis-Napoleon was becoming obsessed with getting more of the British gold. And the miners, whether in New South Scotland or in New New France, were worrying about getting any gold, because it was proving a lot harder to find than they had thought.

Yes, a few people were making it big, and a few large nuggets of gold had been dug up, but it took an awful lot of time to put together enough cornflake-crumb sized pieces of gold to make anything like a nugget.

And to add to their woes, the surface gold was all found very, very quickly, meaning the miners had to dig deeper and deeper searching for it. This meant deep shafts and tunnels all over the landscape, like a giant herd of wombats were building a wombat housing development.

CHAPTER 8

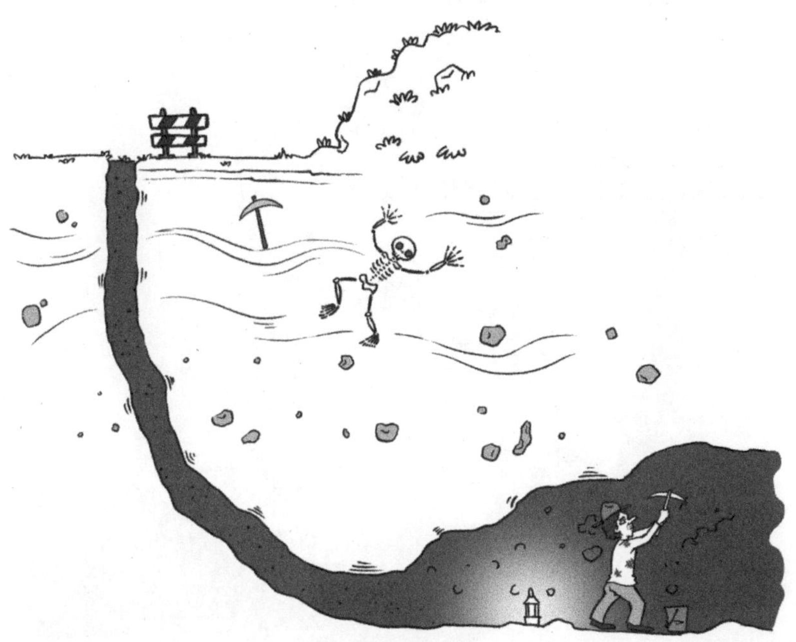

I have to tell you, life on the diggings could be pretty hard. The miners often worked over 12 hours a day, six days a week, digging and sifting through dirt and mud. Many days they wouldn't find anything at all, and at the end of a long day all they had to look forward to was falling asleep on a rough blanket in a leaky canvas tent.

For meals they often had either undercooked or burned damper – made from flour and water – accompanied with salted meat. Fruits and vegetables were in short supply and the drinking water soon became muddied and polluted. And let's not even talk about toilets – though there were enough pits around if you weren't fussy and were good at keeping your balance.

Many of the miners were so bored and lonely they would go looking for a drink in the evenings and would spend what little money they had on grog, and later in the evening there were inevitably fights. Often between people who didn't even speak the same language to know what they were fighting about. Also at night thieves would tip-toe around and try and steal things from your tent. So most diggers had a gun of some sort. And drunken diggers getting into fights and guns were not a good combination.

Then, day after day you did it all over again. Hoping you'd find a bit of gold and hoping it would rain just a bit, but not too much, and hoping nobody would use your mine shaft for a toilet again, and hoping you wouldn't get sick. If you did get sick there was not a lot in the way of medical help. Those visiting the diggings at the time, seeing the poor health and unsanitary conditions, said it was a very, very unhealthy lifestyle – but at least there were a lot of ready holes to use as graves if people died.

Very soon half a million people had arrived in the two colonies searching for gold. And the colonies no longer seemed just French or English-speaking, as people had come from all over the world – Ireland and Sweden and Germany and China and Portugal and South America

– and even from Luxembourg! All the nationalities made life on the diggings a bit crazy, and contributed to communication breakdowns between people, which led to fights and made things very difficult to manage.

Over time more and more women slowly arrived on the goldfields until about 20% of people there were women or girls. They were wives and mothers and teachers or nurses, and it was hoped they would have a good influence on the rough men. Because another thing history teaches us is that if you leave too many men alone in an all-male environment for too long – they go a bit crazy. And add gold fever to that and it's not a good thing.

The damage the miners did to each other when they got into fights was quite high – but the damage they did the land was worse. In the New New France goldfields alone it was estimated that about one metre of topsoil was removed by the miners. Also animals were hunted and rivers and streams were polluted and diverted – all devastating the land.

In fact, the First Nations Dja Dja Wurrung people of central Victoria still refer to the goldfields as 'upside down country'.

Interestingly though, the discovery of gold brought some opportunities for First Nations people. As the settlers quit their jobs and headed to the goldfields, those jobs opened for First Nations people. Yeah, not much consolation for people who had largely been chased off their lands and marginalised though!

CHAPTER 9

T - A - X Spells Licence Fee

But back to the crazy plans each colony came up with steal each other's gold – or at least to stop their gold being taken to the other colony. The French came up with a plan to stop anybody trying to return back across the Border River to New South Scotland with gold. They put guards on the main river crossings, telling diggers they had to spend their gold in the French Colony. So the diggers just used a fraction of their gold to spend on buying small boats and rowed themselves back across the river out of sight of the French guards.

The British then tried a scam that the one of the colonial aides had once fallen for – when a conman told him he could weigh his gold and give him an accurate estimate of its worth. The idea was that they sent spies into New New France with scales and lumps of lead of all sizes painted gold. They would weigh the gold given to them, and would then substitute it for the painted lead, keeping the gold. But yeah, nah, that didn't work either because when they had a nice pile of gold they were robbed by a French bushranger who took it all (And of course the New South Scotland military aide said, 'I told you so!').

The French then sent letters to all foreign miners in New New France saying the letter was from an African Princess who was trying to get a fortune in inheritance out of her country, and if they supplied their bank details they would be sent the inheritance. (This scam is still in use today – ask you parents about it). But again, almost nobody fell for it.

So eventually the administrators in New South Scotland and New New France could not find any other way of getting income from the gold than to start taxing miners. And I think we've been pretty clear on how well miners take to being taxed.

So let's pretend for a minute that you and I are the tax officials and you have to come up with a plan to tax miners that won't cause a revolt. Maybe we would say, 'Let's just put a tax on the gold that is dug up, so you know, the richer get taxed more and those who don't find any gold don't get taxed.' That sounds fair, right?

I mean we wouldn't be stupid enough to say, 'Let's put the same tax on everybody, whether they are finding any gold or not.' That sounds dumb, right? Particularly if we had said to each other, 'Let's call it a licence fee, and not a tax. That way nobody will get upset about it being a tax.'

That sounds even dumber, yeah? History teaches us that people tend to know a tax regardless of what it is called.

And can you guess what they decided? Yep, in New South Scotland the governor implemented a licence fee – which meant that all miners had to buy a licence to dig up gold at a particular location. And only at that location. The licence lasted for a month, and it had to be renewed each month, regardless of whether you had found any gold or not.

Naturally the reaction was not good.

The Turon Rebellion

The first clash between miners and authorities over licence fees was not at the Eureka Stockade in Victoria, but rather at the Sofala goldfield near Turon north of Bathurst in New South Wales.

At first the miners simply crossed the Border River from New South Scotland to New New France to avoid paying the licence fee, but then Louis-Napoleon decided to bring in his own licence fees, and half the diggers went back north again. It all depended on how much each colony was charging for their licence. And as each colony raised the price a little by little, to ensure they were getting more revenue than the other, the miners moved north and south and north again.

Until finally the miners had had enough of licence fees altogether and decided to do something about it!

At first the miners at the goldfield had complied with licence requests, but as heavy rains and flooding halted their work they soon objected to having to pay 30 shillings a month. Added to this, troopers were often very harsh in their enforcement of the licence fees – dragging miners off to jail if they didn't have their licence on them.

Things came to a head in February 1852 when a crowd of several hundred protesting and heavily-armed miners marched along the Turon River calling for more rights for miners. Many of the miners were Irish who had been involved in Ireland's fight for independence and were considered troublesome rebels by the authorities.

They stated they were prepared to offer armed resistance, and it was not until the Government sent in soldiers did the miners back down. The threat of violence did however force the Government to better acknowledge their complaints. Though not nearly enough, as we shall see.

Crazy Taxes

Throughout history there have been some very crazy attempts by governments to come up with taxes to raise money to pay for things (like their own salaries) and even crazier ways for people to avoid paying them. Some of the oddest included:

- In 1660, England placed a tax on fireplaces, which led to people bricking up their fireplaces to avoid paying the tax.
- In 1696, England implemented a window tax, based on the number of windows in a building. It led to many houses bricking up their windows – which became a health problem.

- In the 1700s, England then placed a tax on bricks, so builders started using large bricks so they would need fewer of them.
- In 1712, England next brought in a tax on printed wallpaper, so builders hung plain wallpaper and then painted patterns on it.
- In the 1700s, Russian Emperor Peter the Great placed a tax on beards, hoping to force men to be more clean-shaven, as was common in Western Europe.
- In the late 1700s the French brought in a salt tax which angered so many people it was one of the factors leading to the French Revolution.

CHAPTER 10

El Dorado

Meanwhile, over the borders in the colonies of Nuevo Nuevo Spain, and New New Holland, they were crazily digging up the land everywhere hoping to find gold of their own. Because here is another strange thing about gold, we know that having it can make you lose your common sense and act like a complete idiot, but not having it when somebody else does can make you lose even more common sense and act like an even bigger idiot.

Of course the First Nations people of the whole continent were not overly impressed by this total idiotic behaviour. They had already been pushed off their lands by settlers who wanted to set up farms or graze sheep and cattle. Then they were told that plants and animals were no longer free for the taking – as had been their custom for thousands of years. And on top of all that they were now moved further off their lands with all these crazy people coming and digging holes all over the place, searching for gold.

The ultimate irony is that many First Nations people knew where gold could be found – but they just didn't lose all their common sense and act like complete idiots about it. Which meant that nobody really asked them about it. And if that's not showing a lack of common sense and behaving like a complete idiot – I don't know what is!

After trekking up and down the length of Nuevo Nuevo Spain – the area that is now Queensland – some Spanish miners did eventually find gold. But it was right up the top of the Cape York Peninsula (Or Cape El Dorado, as they now called it), quite some distance inland, in an area that was very hot and dry half the year and then pouring down rain in the other half.

Now we need to push the pause button on the remote and have a bit of interesting backstory. Remember how Captain Cook hit the Great Barrier Reef and his ship sunk, and he never got back to Britain to report on what he had found, so the British were not the first to colonise the land? Well – a few sailors and marines survived the shipwreck and struggled ashore and were eventually made welcome by the local Guugu Yimidhirr people.

I say eventually, because they at first watched these strangers very, very closely to determine if they were spirits of their dead come back to the land or not. They finally decided they were not spirits of their dead, as they did not seem to understand the land and how to find food there. They didn't even seem to know what foods should be eaten in what seasons.

So they wondered if they might be evil spirits – albeit very dumb evil spirits.

But they didn't act like any of the evil spirits in their stories, so maybe they were just people. Dumb people who couldn't feed themselves amongst so much food.

So the Guugu Yimidhirr people took the survivors into their clans and taught them how to live with and understand the land. And the survivors in turn taught them English and taught them about how Europeans understood the world.

Now it may have been that at some point one of the Guugu Yimidhirr people showed one of the survivors a piece of gold that had been traded by the people further inland and the survivors – who now thought of the people here as their family – warned them what would happen when Europeans discovered gold.

Do I need to say it again? They would lose all their common sense and act like idiots.

So here we are in far north Queensland, nearly 100 years after the survivors from the Endeavour shipwreck had been taken in by the clans, and perhaps had children and so on – and Spanish explorers show up looking for gold.

This was the moment that their parents and grandparents had been warning them off. A moment of great derangement upon which the future of their people would hinge.

Putting on our Really Truly Historically Factual hat, ships started appearing at the Endeavour River and they built the town of Cooktown so quickly it appeared to pop up overnight. And suddenly there were thousands of miners arriving and trekking off up into the ranges to look for gold. The First Nations people weren't too happy about this sudden influx of people wanting to stomp all over their land and sacred sites without permission, and taking the food and water and digging up the place.

The Palmer River Goldfield in Cape York, inland from Cooktown, was known as a place where the First Nations peoples were very hostile, and often attacked people crossing their lands – as was the custom in their laws. It was also a difficult place to work, as I said, being either very hot and dry or raining like crazy.

El Dorado

The word El Dorado has come to mean a city of gold that many Spanish searched for in Central and Southern America. The original term was El Hombre Dorado – or The Golden Man. It described a mythical chief who was covered in gold as part of an initiation ceremony.

There may have been some truth in this as a writer in the 17th century, Juan Rodriguez Freyle, told how a local chief in Columbia was covered in gold dust which was then washed off him in a lake while his attendants threw gold at him.

This story slowly changed getting better and better until it became a city, then a kingdom and finally an empire of gold.

So dozens of Spanish explorers trekked all over Central and Southern America looking for this fabled city of gold. The First Nations people figured out pretty quickly that if they told the Spanish explorers that the city existed to the north, or the south, or the west, or anywhere that was not their own territory, the Spanish would head off leaving them in peace.

Naturally no one ever found El Dorado, but if you look it up on a map there is actually a town called El Dorado in Northern Victoria. Needless to say it is not all made of gold.

For the miners, when it rained it uncovered more gold, which was a good thing – but it washed out the roads so supplies could not get through – which was a bad thing. Many miners had to eat their horses or leather saddles as they panned in the mud.

The Palmer River gold find attracted 6,000 miners – of whom 40% were Chinese – but only for a few short years. Almost as suddenly as it was set up, the area was practically deserted when gold ran out.

But let's run our What If filter across that and see what might have happened had the Spanish miners found people at the Endeavour River who understood their crazed desire to get gold, spoke English, and were willing to negotiate a deal?

The Spaniards of course would have been gobsmacked and wanted to know how they had learned English and not Spanish for a start, as every Spaniard knows that Spanish is the best language in the world and English is a jumbled mix of rubbish. But luckily in our telling at least one of the Spaniards spoke enough English to communicate with the Guugu Yimidhirr people.

And the meeting went something like this:

'My boss wants to know how come you speak English?'

'How come he doesn't?' replies one of the locals, sitting down on the ground with the Spanish.

The translator decides it best not to tell his boss that response and asks again, 'Did you learn it from English spies?'

'No. Our ancestors learned it from white men who came to live with us.'

'Missionaries?'

'What are they? They were British sailors whose ship sunk out there.'

'I see. How long ago was this.'

'In the time of my grandfather.'

The translator tells this to his boss in Spanish and the man nods his head and smiles. Then he asks the translator to ask another question.

'Did they claim the land here for Britain?' he asks the elders.

'They lived on the land. They did not need to claim it.'

'I see. So there is no prior claim to the land before us?'

'There is us.'

'But you are savages.'

'No you are savages.'

Again the translator decides not to translate this.

'We want to build a town here so we can reach the goldfields.'

'That is fine.'

The boss sees the way the elders nod their heads and he smiles.

'Good. So you will not attack our miners or anything?'

'No. Of course not.'

'That is excellent.' The translator again tells his boss what has been said and he can see he is looking more and more pleased.

'But you will have to pay a mining tax,' says one of the elders. 'You will need to pay us and all the people whose land you plan to cross or dig up.'

'Oh,' say the translator. He turns to his boss and knows it is going to be a long time before he sees him smile again.

CHAPTER 11

Let's Not Forget the Dutch

And let's not forget the Dutch! They had been sending people all over the colony of New New Holland looking for gold, and they had come back with tin and copper and iron and lead and even silver. But no gold!

The Dutch were greatly disappointed. They could mine those things and export them and make a bit of money of course, but whoever heard of a lead rush, or a tin rush? What was the good of having very sensible copper or silver mine, if they couldn't even demonstrate that their citizens were every bit lacking in common sense and being as idiotic as the citizens of the other colonies?

In desperation the Dutch came up with a cunning plan to buy gold from the Luxembourgers and pretend they had found it on their own land. For they had heard that the Luxembourgers had started mining on lots of the islands off the west coast and were getting very, very rich from it.

So they sent some senior officials to go and buy a box of the Luxembourg gold. And to be fair, when you choose someone for such an important mission, it is probably not a great idea to choose your wife's dopey younger brother that nobody wants to give a job to. There were undoubtedly good reasons nobody wanted to employ him.

But that's what the governor of New New Holland did!

And something clearly got lost in translation, for when he eventually returned to New New Amsterdam with the box of gold and opened it at Government House, the Dutch governor and his aides stared in and found it was full of dried bird poo.

'What is the meaning of this?' the Dutch governor asked his aides.

'War?' asked the military adviser.

'Have they sent us this as an insult?' the Governor demanded of his wife's dopey younger brother.

The man looked a bit confused and said, 'No, no. This is what they are mining on the islands. I saw it myself.'

'Poo?' asked the Governor. 'They are mining poo?'

'Not just any poo,' said his wife's dopey younger brother. 'Bird poo.'

The Governor stared at him and the aides stared at him.

'We sent you to buy some gold,' said the Governor.

'We heard they were becoming very rich,' said one of the aides.

'This is how they are becoming rich,' said the Governor's wife's dopey younger brother.

'By digging up bird poo?'

'No, by selling it.'

'Yes! Selling it to us!' said the Governor, furiously. 'We paid good money for this! It is an outrageous insult. We have more than enough poo of our own in this colony. We have sheep poo and we have cow poo and we have…' He looked around to his aides.

'Chicken poo,' said one of them.

'Pig poo,' said another.

'Yes!' said the Governor. 'Why would we want any more poo?'

'So… should we send them back some of our poo and start trade negotiations?' asked the Governor's wife's dopey younger brother.

Everyone in the room stared at him.

'I think war is perhaps a better idea,' said the Governor. 'If they won't sell us their gold we will invade them and take it.'

But we'll have to get back to the Dutch vs Luxembourg war later, because first we need to talk about race problems on the goldfields.

CHAPTER 12
Chinese

Now while there were a lot of different nationalities all over the land looking for gold, they were predominantly European, with one exception – the Chinese. And not only did the Chinese look different, but they acted differently, had different customs and religions and language.

And I think we all know from our own experiences in school that anybody who is very different tends to get picked on by the bullies of the school, because – well that's complicated. Bullies can be insecure and need to boost their esteem by picking on someone, or they can be afraid of things that are different, or they can just be pig-headed stupid and mean.

And that's pretty much what happened to the Chinese in all the colonies.

At first it wasn't too bad as there weren't too many of them arriving and everybody had a fair chance to find gold. But as more and more Chinese arrived and gold became harder and harder to find, many diggers started resenting the Chinese and blaming them for their lack of success.

And the thing that really got miners upset about the Chinese was that they would come to a mine site that a European miner had abandoned, and work through the dug-up piles of dirt and find gold there. It was a lot of hard work, but Chinese diggers found profit in what European miners had rejected. And the European miners weren't happy about it.

For instance, complaints made against the Chinese miners were that they were dirty – this from diggers who might wash once a week while most Chinese washed with hot water every evening.

Chinese were also accused of using drugs like opium – this from diggers who regularly got drunk every evening.

And they were accused of being gamblers, playing Chinese card and tile games. This from diggers who had a reputation for regularly losing all their money in other forms of gambling.

They were also accused of taking gold out of the colonies and not spending it here as many diggers did. Many millions of pounds worth of gold really was taken back to China –contributing greatly to Chinese economic growth at the time.

But it was very difficult being a Chinese miner in any of the colonies at this time. They had come from provinces in southern China where there were many wars and troubles like famine, and they had come to make money for their families. This meant a wealthy warlord or merchant had lent them money to come to the colonies, and they would have to pay that money back with interest before they could earn any money for their families.

They travelled out on ships in conditions that were overcrowded and harsh and when they landed in one of the colonies they had to walk to the diggings – often in long lines of men walking single file, carrying their possessions on either side of a bamboo pole.

The Governments even found ways to add extra taxes to the Chinese miners, demanding that each Chinese person who arrived needed to pay £10. This was a lot of money for people with little savings, and who hadn't started earning any income yet. As a result ships landed Chinese miners outside the borders of the colony, and they had to walk overland several hundred miles to avoid paying the tax.

There were also very few Chinese women on the goldfields at first – and not that many later on – so life was difficult and lonely. Putting on our Really Truly Historically Factual hat, in 1857 there were an estimated 25,000 Chinese men and only three Chinese women on all the diggings.

Things had improved a little by 1861 when there were 38,000 men and 11 women! Okay, maybe not such an improvement.

(Though we should remember that was 38,000 different men with 38,000 different stories and background and families and motives, as much as it was 11 different women, all with different stories and backgrounds and families and motives too).

To add to their problems the diggers began treating them more and more harshly. They were first seen as oddities, then they were seen as rivals for gold, and then they were seen as threats to the diggers and to the colonies.

And we should remember that back in the 1850s your average European thought that they were more superior to any other people and that Chinese were somehow inferior to them. Racism isn't based on common sense, and when you add gold fever's impact and idiocy on top of it, you get a lot of bad racist behaviour.

The first signs of trouble began in 1853 when there were anti-Chinese riots at the Turon River in New South Wales. You might remember the goldfields here, north of Bathurst, had also been the sight of the first anti-licence fee rebellion, so clearly there were a lot of troublemakers there.

This was followed by riots at Bendigo and then the Buckland River, near Mount Buffalo, in Victoria, in 1857. At that time there were about 2,000 Chinese compared to about 700 Europeans in the area. On 4 July about 100 miners left a large meeting at the local hotel where they decided to throw the Chinese miners off the goldfields. Newspapers of the time reported that the miners were led by drunken Americans who had been celebrating US Independence Day.

The men attacked the Chinese camps, burning down their tents and places of worship, beating and robbing them of their gold and possessions. The European wife of one Chinese miner was beaten and nearly killed, while another Chinese miner had his finger cut off to steal his gold ring. It was never recorded how many died of the violence, or from exposure in the bush as they fled for their lives, though many were sheltered by sympathetic European diggers or landowners.

Police later arrested 13 men involved in the rioting, but the European jury let most of them go.

It was not sending a good message to other miners, and similar riots occurred at Meroo (1854) Rocky River (1856) Tambaroora (1858) Kiandra (1860) and Nundle (1861).

Things got so bad that the Chinese set up their own goldfield near Ararat in Victoria. But they were even driven off that. Europeans heard about it and soon flocked to the goldfield, to find the Chinese had the best claims already.

There were many violent incidents in which Chinese miners were attacked and driven off their claims.

All in all, it was not so great to be a Chinese person on the goldfields – so let's put on our What If glasses and look at history from a different angle. What if that goldfield that the Chinese discovered in Ararat in regional New New France had so many Chinese there that they threw the Europeans off?

Let's consider how things might have been the other way around.

So the Chinese found the gold and at first passed messages only to other Chinese people, not letting Europeans know about the gold find. Then as more and more Chinese arrived they started building more permanent houses than tents, and their temples and stores were also made of wood with roofs and proper doors.

Lambing Flat Anti-Chinese Riots

The most notorious of all anti-Chinese riots occurred at Lambing Flat, near Young, in New South Wales, in 1860-61. There was actually a series of anti-Chinese protests – often led by criminals or thugs.

The worse riot occurred in June 1861, when several thousand angry miners attacked about two thousand Chinese. The miners were supported by a brass band and flew a large hand-painted flag that had written on it, "Roll Up" and "No Chinese", centred around a southern cross.

A European miner at the time wrote:

"... with yells and hoots, hunted and whipped the Chinamen, knocking them down with the butt ends of their whips... in many cases pulling their pig tails out by the roots, and planting their fresh trophies on their banners. Not satisfied with this, their next step was to rifle through the tents for hidden gold, and then deliberately fire every tent in the encampment."

Many of the Chinese were able to get shelter on the nearby property of the kindly Roberts family.

Police were sent to the goldfield to restore order – and three miners were arrested for their part in the riots. Only three! And even then about 1,000 miners surrounded the small police camp and demanded their freedom. The police were able to disperse the miners after exchanging gun fire and making a surprise change by the mounted troops. But the police then felt it wiser to sneak off to nearby Yass.

The Government then sent a force of 280 soldiers, sailors and extra police from Sydney to ensure more violence did not break out.

Just one rioter, William Spicer, was convicted, and two unconvicted rioters were later elected to parliament.

All the buildings were laid out in neat rows and the Chinese had organised their own law-enforcement groups to keep the peace.

Whenever a European gold miner came near they told him that they were building vegetable gardens in the town as there was a lot of money to be made from selling vegetables to the miners across the colony.

So far so good, right, but sooner or later the word was going to get out that the Chinese had found gold, and the Chinese knew that this was likely to happen too. So in this version of history the Chinese had done a deal with the French Government. In return for paying some gold taxes they would be protected by the authorities.

Well, as predicted, the story soon got out to European miners that there was a really good goldfield at Ararat, and they started showing up in big numbers. Imagine the shock of the first European miners to arrive to find they were way outnumbered by Chinese who told them that they could only stay on the goldfields if they went to distant locations where there was not much water nor likely any gold.

The European miners didn't like this one bit, of course, and wanted to protest it, but as long as there were more Chinese than them it made it a bit hard to do anything about it. So they waited their time, as more and more Europeans showed up. And finally the key troublemakers figured they had enough men to throw the Chinese off their claims and steal them.

So they followed the usual formula – getting drunk and rowdy and getting a big crowd together and whooping them up into a fury, telling them how unfair it was that the Chinese had all the best gold claims, and they were taking gold that rightly should be theirs, and they needed to be shown who was boss!

The miners then formed up into a mob and set off to attack the Chinese camp. But as they reached the outskirts they found a line of French troopers there, determined to protect the Chinese.

The Europeans were outraged and called on the troopers to join them. But the troopers had their orders – which was to follow the golden rule (which in this case is, whoever has the gold makes the rules!). When the miners started throwing rocks at the troopers they attacked, chasing the miners all over the goldfields on their horses. Some had their hair cut off by troopers' bayonets or swords and many hid in mineshafts, begging for mercy.

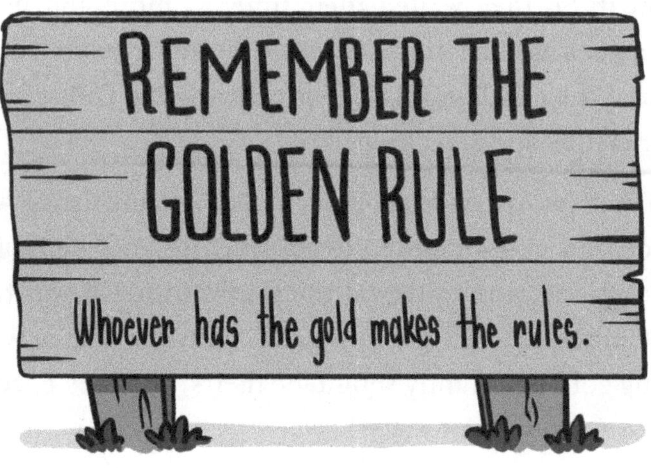

Many fled to a nearby property to seek shelter, but the French property owner had a trade deal with the Chinese and told them to get off his property or they would be charged with trespass.

The upset miners petitioned the French Government to compensate them for their losses – but Louis-Napoleon determined that the only losses they had sustained was to their dignity and they were lucky not to be fined for disturbing the peace.

(It is something you can do to many incidents in history. Turn the story around and just see how you feel about it when roles are reversed.)

CHAPTER 13

Dealing With the Chinese Question

And things were not going much smoother back in New South Scotland. If you remember almost all the gold that had been discovered was on Wiradjuri land, and the Wiradjuri controlled access to the goldfields.

And when it came to the disputes that were happening between Chinese miners and European ones, the First Nations people only had to ask which group had been the most racist to them? And which had been the most insulting? And which had wanted to throw them off their lands to get at their gold? Yep – the Europeans.

So they tended to favour the Chinese miners, which was not pleasing the hard-lined racist yobbo miners at all. You could imagine the debate being had in the Governor's office with his top aides.

'So we have a problem with the miners protesting about their access to the goldfields,' says the Governor.

'But if they are not on the goldfields, they are not miners yet, strictly speaking, yes?' asks his top aide, while she sews up a hole in his socks. Yet another of her many talents.

'Well, I suppose that is true,' says the Governor, 'But they would very much like to be gold miners and they are complaining that the Wiradjuri people will not give them enough access to goldfields.'

'What is it they actually want from us?' asks the administrative aide.

'I gather they want us to tear up the treaty with the Wiradjuri, allowing them full access to the lands,' says the military aide. 'And that would have some advantages, you know.'

'Would it?' asks the Governor.

'Well yes. It would stop all the other pesky local people demanding treaties too, and it would stop all the farmers protesting their limited access to lands and it would remind everybody that this is our colony!'

'You can't just tear up a treaty,' says the top aide.

'Of course we can,' says the military aide. 'We're British! We do that sort of thing all the time.'

'Are you sure you are not being influenced in this argument by your own shares in gold mining companies?' the top aide asks him, examining the fixed sock.

'Why should that even be something to consider?' he asks. 'We are British administrators. It is our job to personally benefit from being in charge of things.'

The top aide sighs and shakes her head.

'Hmm,' says the Governor. 'I can see this is going to be a tricky matter to decide on. Perhaps best if we hold it over to our next meeting.'

'And then there is the Chinese question,' says the administrative aide.

'Which question is that?' asks the Governor. 'And is the question in Chinese? I don't actually speak Chinese.'

'No, no,' says the administrative aide. 'The question of the Chinese miners. We have also received many protests about the number of Chinese on the goldfields. The miners say they are dirty and gamble and waste water.'

'How can they be both dirty and also waste water?' asks the Governor. 'Surely if they were too clean they'd be wasting water?'

'I don't know all the details,' says the administrative aide. 'But the miners are not happy about the number of Chinese miners.'

'Not happy indeed,' says the military aide. 'I suggest we tear up the treaty, send in the troops to occupy the goldfields, chase the Chinese away and sign some contracts with major mining companies.'

CHAPTER 13

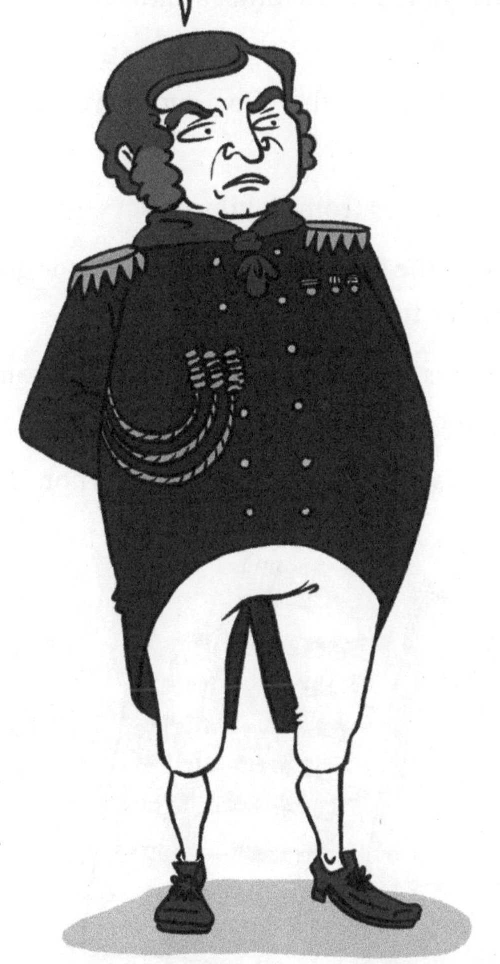

'Like your mining company?' the top aide asks.

'We'll be selling shares,' he says to her. 'There's a tidy fortune to be made.'

'More likely a messy fortune,' she says. 'You do know the British Government has signed an agreement with China giving each other's citizens certain rights and protection?'

'Have they?' asks the Governor. 'Where did you read that?'

'In the dispatches from London.'

'Hmm,' says the Governor. 'I can see this is going to be a tricky matter to decide on.'

'Let me guess,' says the top aide. 'Perhaps you'd like us to hold it over to our next meeting?'

'A splendid suggestion,' says the Governor. 'Now what about tea?'

CHAPTER 14

Planning to Invade

So things were getting very tense between all the colonies and the governments of each were getting crazier and crazier, trying to find ways to get each other's gold. And history teaches us that when one country has something that another country wants, there is a traditional way of solving the problem.

They invade!

And sure enough, each colony had their best military aides draw up possible invasion plans (well, to be fair the word "best" here is only relative to who was living in the colony at the time).

The French planned to cross the Border River northwards and take possession of the New South Scotland goldfields.

The British were going to cross the Border River southwards to take possession of the New New France goldfields.

The Spanish were going to build a giant Armada and sail it down to Sydney during the worst time of year and have it wrecked in a storm.

The Dutch were going to send their troops to the Luxembourg mines to find out how they were getting so rich – certain they were digging up gold, and not bird poo.

And only the Luxembourgers were in no rush to invade anyone, making plenty of money from their bird poo mining. Like the Dutch they had vainly searched for gold all along the coast, and like the Dutch they found there was little chance of a gold rush anywhere there. But they did find bird poo that triggered a poo rush.

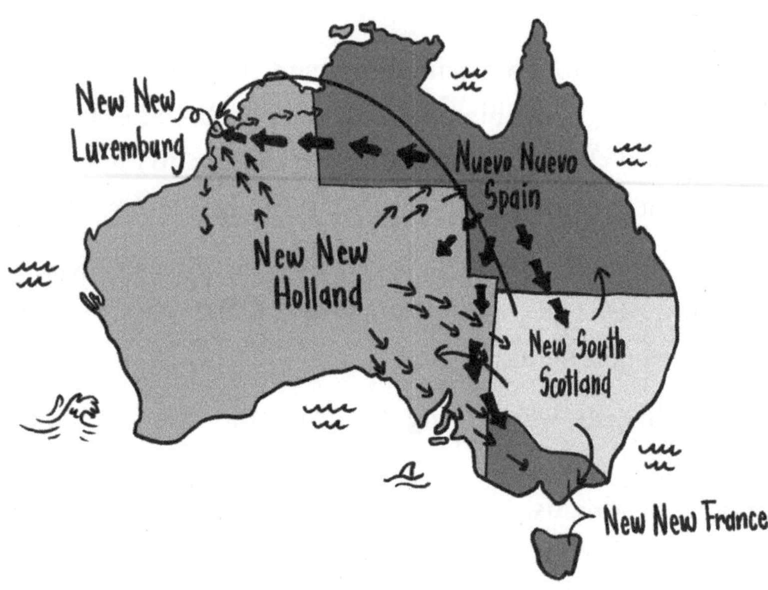

The Luxembourgers found that many of the offshore islands down south were absolutely covered in bird poo. Knee deep and more. Now you might be wondering how that was a good thing – but bird poo (which is known as guano) is very valuable as a fertiliser for crops.

And there really was a poo rush with lots of different companies trying to stake out the best bird poo locations to mine it and sell it.

Like the goldfields, the poo fields were often very hard work (and smelly), with the miners living in remote locations with poor food and shelter.

The main difference I believe was that nobody had plans to make jewellery and clothing ornaments nor horseshoes out of bird poo! But it did make the Luxembourgians very rich, very quickly, even if the Dutch did not understand how.

Okay, back to the invasions.

CHAPTER 15

An Australian Civil War

Well, back to the invasion soon, because first I want a quick word about how we think about the past and the different ways it might play out. In the USA there are lot of alternate histories based around what if the South won the Civil War (as there are a lot of Civil War crazies who dress up in uniforms and re-enact the civil war each year, pretending to be soldiers at the time).

So naturally some alternate historians have asked the question – What If Australia had a civil war? How might that look.

It's a tricky question to ask, as it is hard to find exact parallels with the USA Civil War. They had a natural divide already between the industrialised North and the agricultural South. The South relied on slaves from Africa to work the fields, while the North did not. So when Europe started looking at slavery and saying – 'You know, this is actually a pretty terrible idea', the rich farmers in the South just put their heads down and pretended they couldn't hear them.

Slavery was abolished in the United Kingdom in 1833, but in the USA those who were getting rich from slaves just kept their heads down and kept their slaves in the fields. So the USA became divided over the issue of slavery which reinforced the divide between the North and the South. Along with some other crazy politics, this led slowly to the Civil War breaking out.

Anyway, to have a similar thing happen in Australia it is possible to turn things upside down and say that the state of Queensland in the north was like the South in the USA, as they had significant numbers of slaves working the farms that had been kidnapped from the Pacific Island. This was known as "blackbirding" and they were largely taken from the islands of Vanuatu and

Solomon Islands, closest to Australia, but also from Fiji and Papua New Guinea.

Between 1863 and 1904, 62,000 South Sea Islanders were brought to Australia to work in the sugar industry, cutting sugar cane. Many had been tricked aboard ships and kidnapped. In fact there was one unfortunate incident when the Anglican Bishop of Melanesia, John Patterson, was killed by locals on the island of Nukapu in the Solomon Islands. Blackbirders had come to the island a few days previously and kidnapped five people. Considering the Church often tried to convince young men to go with them to their missions, it is likely the locals didn't see any difference and wanted to show very clearly what they thought of having their young people taken away.

You might read in some books that we never had slavery in Australia, but I think you'll find the descendants of those people who were taken from the Pacific Islands disagree. Technically many were called "indentured labourers" – which means they had to work for little pay for a set period and were then turned free. But I also think, practically, you'll find there was little difference between that and being a slave.

Many First Nations people were also working in slave conditions on properties, with strict conditions and little pay, if any.

So we could have the States of the South in Australia prepared to go to war with Queensland over slavery and other crazy political things. (The very first State of Origin battle, if you are a rugby fan). But there are a few other things we'd need to change to make this idea work. For instance, the population of Queensland was very small compared to that of New South Wales and Victoria – largely because of the gold rushes – so if there was a Civil War in Australia it would probably be over in a few weeks because there were so many more people in the South.

So we should use our What If superpowers to change things around a bit, and increase the population of Queensland to make it a bit more equal.

The next question we'd have to ask is, would Australians really fight each other? Well back in the 19th century there was no single country called Australia, and people felt a very strong identity with the colony they lived in. So there was enough healthy competition and jealousy between colonies to make that realistic.

But would the people of the time actually get into a military uniform and be prepared to fight to end or defend slavery? Well, probably they would. The first rule of going to war for any government is to make the war about something else. Most wars in history have really been about territory or resources or political differences, but the soldiers were told they were about freedom or defeating evil.

For instance, in the USA very few landowners who had slaves actually fought in the war. The average Confederate soldier from the South was fairly poor and believed they were fighting against Yankee aggression. Those dastardly northern states wanted to take over the South and change the way they lived! Or so they were told by the landowners who owned slaves and wanted to protect that way of life.

And there were strong streaks of freedom amongst colonial Australians. So maybe it would be possible to imagine lines and lines of soldiers from the Southern Colonies facing up against lines and lines of soldiers from Queensland, each fighting to end or to defend their 'ways of life'. While the rich landowners and politicians in either colony made more and more money from the sale of leather and meat and wool and guns and boots and everything else you need to fight a civil war.

But what would trigger the war? Here's a thing about most conflicts, they are often triggered by one crazy incident that could well have been avoided. In the USA there was an absolutely crazy guy known as John Brown, who largely triggered the Civil War. He was very religious and believed his mission in life was to stop slavery, and with his sons he behaved like a bushranger, attacking people who supported slavery. He said slavery would never be ended by words, but only by action!

The peak of his crazy ideas happened at a place called Harper's Ferry in the state of Virginia. He had a plan to raid all the guns at the armoury there and start a rebellion in which all the slaves would rise up and join him and fight for their freedom.

CHAPTER 15

John Brown

Unfortunately, when he attacked the armoury the slaves of the area didn't rise up and join him. Like many crazy political leaders his vision of what would happen didn't actually align with the vision of most people around him.

It's pretty easy to imagine a similar thing happening in Australia. Let's give our John Brown the name of Bruce Smith. And Bruce is a religious fanatic who believes that kidnapping workers from the Pacific Islands is just wrong and needs to be abolished. He also believes that all the political delegations coming up to Brisbane from Sydney to seek a peaceful way to end slavery are not making any difference.

So he has a plan. He is going to travel up to Rockhampton in disguise, with a handful of his followers and they are going to raid the military armoury there and trigger an uprising of the local South Sea Islanders.

But it also doesn't work out, for different reasons.

Firstly, the armoury at Rockhampton only has a few pistols and a rifle. Not even enough to go around his gang. Secondly, when they raid the armoury, it is a Sunday morning, and most people are sleeping in and don't even notice. Thirdly, there is a cricket match on that day in town – and if comes to a choice between sport and a rebellion, you know which one is going to win!

CHAPTER 15

Bruce Smith

~~John Brown~~

So while John Brown was overwhelmed by local forces and captured in the USA, in Rockhampton Bruce Smith sits around the armoury all day waiting for somebody to notice him. And one by one his followers sneak away to watch the cricket until he is left there on his own.

He decides to act and goes down to the cricket oval and takes the umpire hostage, telling everyone that he won't let him go until all the slaves are freed. And that's more than anyone is willing to accept. Disrupting a sporting event!

So Queensland declares this an attack on its way of life, and the rich landowners tell the locals that it threatens their freedom to play cricket and they declare war on the South.

But that's another story...

CHAPTER 16

The Frequently Fairly Ferocious and Fantastically Formidable French Forces

Alright, finally we are back to our story of New South Scotland going to war with New New France. The military aides of both the French and British colonies were very, very excited about it of course. They were convinced this would not only end all those years and years of French versus British rivalry, but would make way for their colony to eventually control the whole continent.

Louis-Napoleon started dressing up like his grandfather, Napoleon 1.0, and walking around the place with his hand tucked into his jacket. He had all the troops assembled and had them practise shouting, 'Vive L'Empereur!' (long live the Emperor!).

Louis-Philippe was not impressed with the way he was behaving, but thought that if the invasion of New South Scotland was a failure, then he would surely be able to finally take over the colony of New New France. Surely.

He watches the way that Louis-Napoleon drills his soldiers and realises that while he has the Napoleon name, he has clearly not inherited Napoleon's military genius. His main strategy is to have the men all fire their weapons at once, and then stand around for a minute or so trying to reload quickly.

It would not take a military genius to figure out that all the British would have to do would be to lie down when the order to fire was given so that the shells and musket balls would go over their heads, and then run and fire at the French while they were reloading at the same time.

So he tells Louis-Napoleon, 'Brilliant! Absolutely brilliant! The British will be shaking in their boots when they see our soldiers and that combined firepower will overwhelm them.'

For an old guy who didn't know how to dab Louis-Philippe had some clever ideas.

And Louis-Napoleon is as vain as any ruler and says, 'Well, thank you very much for saying so. Yes, I think our men are looking fairly formidable.'

'Fairly ferocious and formidable,' says Louis-Philippe.

'Frequently fairly ferocious and fantastically formidable,' agrees Louis-Napoleon.

'Functionally frequently fairly ferocious and fantastically formidable,' says Louis-Philippe after a slight pause.

And Louis-Napoleon responds with, 'Faultlessly functionally frequently fairly ferocious and fantastically factually formidable French.'

Louis-Philippe is unable to think of any more useful f-words except for 'failure' and 'fatal', so he bows his head to the Emperor, or the King, whoever he is today and congratulates him on his clever word play.

But he is thinking to himself, Just as well he is good at word play, so he will still feel he is good at something when he finds out just how rubbish he is at commanding a battle.

CHAPTER 17

The Perfectly Pompous and Practically Pathetic British Plans

And in New South Scotland, the British military aide started dressing up like the Duke of Wellington, who had defeated Napoleon 1.0 at the Battle of Waterloo. The Governor was too preoccupied with drawing and redrawing maps of what the colony would look like after they had defeated the French to spend much time playing dress-ups.

The planning meetings were, as you would expect, a little bit chaotic.

The Governor sits at a table with his maps spread out before him. He has been drawing bridges over the Border River for the British troops to cross. But his top aide – who is today knitting a Rule Britannia beanie for the Governor to wear when he goes into combat – says,

'Excuse me, but couldn't the French troops use those bridges to invade us?'

The Governor looks at the map in horror. 'By Jingo, you're correct. Don't worry, I'll fix it.' And he leans down and draws One Way signs on all the bridges. 'That should solve that problem,' he says.

The Military aide then leans in close and coughs, then again, and then once more – and just before everyone asks if he has some nasty infection, he waves his hands around to get their attention. 'I have an alternative plan,' he says, 'that I think will surprise you by the genius in its planning.'

'Yes, that would surprise me,' says the top aide, looking at him over her knitting.

'Well, what is it?' asks the Governor. 'If it is genius then we certainly want to hear it.'

'You are all aware of the great defeat the British inflicted upon the French at the Battle of Waterloo?' he asks.

'I think the Prussians actually defeated the French at Waterloo,' says the top aide. 'The British were in great danger of being defeated if the Prussians had not arrived late in the day.'

'Be that as it may,' says the military aide, 'what if we were to lure the French army all the way up to Sydney and confront them at the suburb of Waterloo?'

The Governor and the top aide stare at him. 'Do you mean to actually let the French onto our soil?' the Governor asks. 'And to let them advance all the way to just down the road?'

The military aide senses this is not going quite the way he had imagined it would. 'Yes, but the name. I mean Waterloo. How could we lose?'

'And you'd let the French troops raid and pillage all over the colony to get here?' asks the Governor.

'Well, perhaps, um…' says the military aide, tugging at his collar which he suddenly finds is very tight around his neck.

'And if we happened to fight them to a stalemate,' suggests the top aide, 'they'd have half the colony in their possession?'

'Well, not quite half,' the military aide says softly.

'Oh wait on, you're right,' she says. 'The Prussians will come and save us.'

'Umm,' says the military aide, who was never good at recognising sarcasm, 'that isn't very likely, is it?'

The Governor stares at the military aide in great disappointment. 'I think we might just stick with my one-way bridge signs.'

CHAPTER 18

Reaching the Border River

So this is how things play out. The French forces march slowly northwards along tracks and dirt roads and Louis-Napoleon asks his aides why there is no railroad heading north and insists they need to build one at once.

His aides make all these excuses about not needing a railroad heading north, as all the railroads head to the goldfields where they are most needed. But Louis-Napoleon waves his hands at them in annoyance, as if they are pesky flies. And to be truthful there are quite a few pesky flies buzzing around him as well.

This is the first time he has ventured so far out of New New Paris to tour his realm and he finds it is not actually what he had expected. He had somehow thought it would be a lot more like the pictures he had in his residence of rural France, with lots of hedges and happy peasants smiling at him as he rode past. Instead there are endless gum trees and bushland and dirt-poor farmers who stare at him while they pick their noses or brush away flies.

CHAPTER 18

And while he believed he was crossing the realm of New New France, he was actually crossing the land of the Woiworung, the Taungurong, and the Waveroo peoples. Not that he sees too many of the local people, as they have enough sense to hide when they see a large column of soldiers heading their way.

As they set up camp for the night and put up his very ornate tent, and lay down nice rugs and assemble his four-poster bed, he sits with his aides around a table and looks at his campaign map. He has drawn a straight-line heading northeast from New New Paris to the Border River.

'Where are we on the map?' he asks.

His aides look around at the landscape in confusion and each tries to guess where they might be. But the fact is they have never ventured far outside New New Paris either, and are also quite surprised that the landscape doesn't look much like the pictures of France they have in their own homes.

'I believe we are here, your excellency,' says the military aide, always wanting to appear to know what is going on.

Louis-Napoleon makes some measures with his fingers. 'So we should reach the Border River the day after tomorrow, yes?'

The military aide looks around nervously, 'Um, yes, unless we encounter any difficulties.'

'Such as?' Louis-Napoleon asks.

'Well, we might run out of caviar or truffles, and need to send somebody back to New New Paris to fetch more.'

But Louis-Napoleon waves his hand in the air again. The military aide looks around for any flies that he might be shooing, and then realises he is waving his hand at his comment. 'This is war. We must be prepared for some hardships!'

'Of course,' say his aides.

'How are our supplies lasting?' Louis-Napoleon asks.

'We have enough to feed the troops until we reach the Border River,' says one of his aides. 'After that we will be pillaging and looting to feed our men as we advance in to New South Scotland.'

Louis-Napoleon looks around the bushland about them and says, 'I certainly hope they have more farms on their side of the river than we have here.'

◆◆◆

It actually takes them three more days to reach the Border River, which has the military aide coming up with a long list of excuses as to why the map was wrong, and the road was in the wrong place and so on. Louis-Napoleon has a clear plan as to what will happen next. They will camp on the banks of the river and his engineers will build two or three bridges over the river, and when they are complete his army will invade New South Scotland and march towards the goldfields there, stopping only to destroy any army sent against him.

He has read his grandfather's memoirs and learned all his battle strategies off by heart, so that he is certain he will be able to be as great a military genius as he was. And the first rule, he knows, is to take the enemy by surprise.

So he is very upset when they reach the banks of the Border River to see the enemy have just arrived on the opposite bank and are staring in surprise at the French troops.

CHAPTER 18

•••

Of course, the British army's march south went very, very much like the French army's march north. The Governor and his top military aide did not have as nice a tent and a four-poster bed though. Otherwise, very similar.

The men had marched in a long, long line and the Governor had looked at the open plains and bushland and wondered why it was not more like that back home in Britain. Or at least in South Scotland!

He was also a bit surprised by the scarce number of farms they passed. Somehow in his mind the British had settled every corner of the colony, not just around Sydney and the goldfields and a few coastal towns.

But his aides promised him that this great military expedition would see townships springing up all along the path they had travelled and in the future it would be known as the Victory Highway. The Governor quite like the sound of that. Almost as much as naming it after himself.

Each night he consulted his maps with his aides and they showed him where they were each day – well roughly where they were as they weren't much better at navigating than their French counterparts. They would reach the Border River, and the men would rest a day or so while they built bridges across the river and then they would march onwards to the French goldfields. And for that part of the way they had loyal British subjects who had worked on the goldfields to show them the way so that would not get lost. (Well actually they had a few failed miners who had not made any money on the French goldfields, but were willing to charge high prices to show the British troops where it was that they had not made any money).

And once they crossed the river, they would live off the land, raiding French farms for food for the troops. The Governor hoped they had more farms on the French side of the river than they had on the British side, though, as there was not enough on this side to feed an army.

So the men marched. The Governor and his aides rode in a carriage and each day they got closer to the Border River where they would enter enemy territory and their great campaign would be written up by historians as one of the greatest victories of the British Empire. And to ensure that, the Governor had brought along a few historians with him, so he could dictate to them each night what they should be writing about the campaign.

Now here's a thing about governments and history – traditionally governments always prefer history is written in a way that reflects very well on them, detailing all the great things they do and neglecting to mention any of the dumb things they do.

But the thing about historians is, they prefer to write what they believe really happened, and not what the government wants them to write. This means that many governments go to great lengths to hide the records of things that don't reflect well on them so that historians can't tell those stories. But historians do have a habit of finding them anyway and writing them up.

So if you read history books that go back over time you will find that new things are always being discovered and new stories of the past are being told, particularly in areas of history that were covered up or not acknowledged well in the past. These include treatment of First Nations peoples and women's and children's histories and the stories of those who were not in government.

For example while the Governor and the British troops believed they were crossing the territory of New South Scotland, they were actually crossing the lands of the Dharug, Gundungurra, Ngunawal, and southern Wiradjuri peoples.

***

Anyway – I'm guessing you can guess what happens next. The British finally reach the Border River and are surprised to see the French arriving on the other side, staring back at them just as stupidly as they are staring at the French.

The Governor is outraged, of course, as this has upset all his great plans of sneaking into New New France and catching the French by surprise.

'What should we do?' asks the military aide.

'Bring up the engineers,' says the Governor. 'And don't forget those one-way signs!'

CHAPTER 19

Another Grand Idea

Well things played out then pretty much as you'd expect they played out. The French and the British taunted each other from either side of the river while the engineers very, very slowly planned out their bridges and very, very slowly began building them. For as soon as the French started building a bridge the British would start one opposite it. And as soon as the British started a bridge the French would start one opposite it too.

And none of the engineers wanted to join the bridges and be attacked by the enemy soldiers. Which meant there were all these half-finished bridges along the river.

But the French had a Grand Idea (or une grande idée, as Louis-Napoleon described it). Having studied his grandfather's military successes he knew that the best way to win victory against an enemy was to flank it. All this really meant was to go around it and attack from the side or the rear. Looking at his maps that meant he would need to send half his troops to the east so that they could find where the Border River started and go around it – hopefully not even getting their feet wet.

Because he knew that no matter how large a river, it had to begin somewhere as just a trickle of a stream. And if they could go around the starting point of the river they could go around the British army and sneak up on them from the side or the rear.

***

Now you've probably guessed this too, but the Governor and his aides were having pretty much the same conversation in their tents. If they went to the east they would find the source of the Border River and they could go around it and blah blah blah – you know how the rest goes.

Well, as a military plan it wasn't too bad, but there were a few things wrong with it that they didn't know at the time. Firstly, it was getting on towards winter by the time the two armies had reached the river and come up with the flanking idea, and to the east were some fairly tall mountains. And it could get very cold in those mountains in winter.

But as they had no really good maps of what the land was like to the east, they had no idea they were sending men up into such difficult terrain.

Louis-Napoleon had done his homework right in studying up on his grandfather's great victories – but he should have also studied up on his great failures. The worst of which was Napoleon's invasion of Russia in 1812. He was as much defeated by the Russian winter as he was by the Russian troops. They let the French come deep into their territory, falling back before him, and burning all the land around the French as they went.

The French even reached the Russian capital of Moscow – and you'd think that would be a great victory, yes? But the Russians had all fled and the French were left with an empty city to wave their flags over. Then the city caught fire. No one is certain if the Russians did this or the French did it by mistake, but much of the city burned down as winter approached.

Then the French had to turn around and flee back through the burned-out empty countryside where there was no food or animals to feed the army, and the terrible Russian winter froze them as they went.

He had gone to Russia with over 500,000 troops and got back to France with only about 100,000. Needless to say, it was not Napoleon's greatest moment.

So under cover of darkness half of the French and British troops snuck out of camp and made their way off towards the east. Now we should admit here that even if this was attempted in Europe, it would also be a dumb idea to try and find the source of the river and go around it – because that would invariably be up in the mountains and very hard to reach.

But the colonial mindset of the time was framed by a certain way of thinking. One was that the colonies here had much nicer weather than in Europe, and also that if Napoleon had been able to cross the Alps to invade northern Italy then surely they could cross the tiny Australian Alps.

But if you've ever been hiking in the Australian Alps in winter, you'll know that it is very, very cold. There can be a lot of ice and snow and if you don't have proper clothing and food and shelter – you are in big trouble.

The Murray River

The first Europeans to see the Murray River were the ill-matched explorers Hamilton Hume and William Hovell. They undertook an expedition to find an overland path from Sydney to Melbourne, and the modern-day Hume Highway is pretty much where their return path was.

They came to the Murray River in 1824 and had a fight about how to cross it. In the end they wrapped canvas around one of their carts and made a boat out of it. This helped them cross the river, but didn't stop the fighting between the two men – who argued all the way down to Melbourne and back again.

The river was next seen by the explorer Charles Sturt who had been travelling down the Murrumbidgee and didn't realise it was the same river that Hamilton and Hume had seen, and named the Hume River. He named it the Murray, after the then British Secretary of State, Sir George Murray. Sturt travelled all the way down the river to South Australia where it enters the sea.

The river became the natural border between the colonies of New South Wales and Victoria, and at first the only way to cross it was by boat – until the first bridge was built in 1879. Eventually train tracks were laid to the river from both sides, but they used different width tracks, so it was not possible to take the same train from Melbourne to Sydney.

The source of the Murray River, up near Mount Kosciusko, is known as Indi Springs, and was located in 1869. There are in fact three key springs that give rise to the Murray River, and from there it flows over 2,500 kilometres until it reaches the sea in South Australia. This makes it is the third longest navigable river in the world, after the Amazon River and the Nile River.

And of course that is exactly what happened. The higher the two armies went into the mountains the smaller and sparser the trees became, so there was not even shelter from the cold wind, nor enough wood to make fires. And they got lost and split up from each other in the rain and they were completely miserable.

The French army actually gave up first and they looked just like pictures you might see of Napoleon's retreat from Russian, all strung out in a long line with their coats wrapped up tight about them, trying to keep warm while struggling through the snow. When the first men returned the French military aide was convinced they had been attacked by a larger force and these lucky few had managed to escape.

When he found they were in fact defeated by the landscape and the weather he was furious.

It wasn't much better for the British, but rather than turning back, they got completely lost and while they thought they were heading back to the main army they were in fact continuing further to the east. To their surprise they came out of the mountains where they could see the sea.

The officers consulted their maps which didn't make much sense to them and finally consulted a member of the Yuin people who had come to see what these cold and hungry soldiers were doing on their land.

'Where are we?' the officers asked the man, making hand signals and pointing at the map.

He looked at them carefully and then pointed at the map and said, 'Yuin land.' But in his own Dhurga language.

This didn't help the British very much so they sent out some scouts and one of them eventually found a settler who had been living in the mountains by himself, very happy to have a corner of the world where no one would disturb him. He was not impressed to find several hundred British soldiers on his doorstep asking for directions.

'Excusez-moi,' said one of the officers in his best French (which admittedly was not great). 'Est-ce la nouvelle nouvelle France?'

'What?' asked the old man. 'Do you speak any English?'

'Um… yes,' said the officer. 'I just want to know if this is New New France?'

The settler looked around him. Up at the sky. Down at his feet. Around to the east and then to the west. 'No, it ain't,' he finally said.

'Oh dear,' said the officer. 'I think we're going to be in a spot of trouble when we get back.'

CHAPTER 20

Eureka!

Yes, of course both the French and the British troops were in trouble when they finally got back to the main forces of their armies. They had failed in their mission and both armies had now run out of food. There was nothing for it but to retreat – tell everyone it was actually a victory - and hope that nobody let the historians know what really happened.

It was a very long and hungry trip back to their capital cities, for of course they could not plunder and pillage their own subjects – so like a lot of equally depressed explorers before them, the soldiers had to cook up their own boots to eat.

Louis-Philippe was waiting eagerly for Louis-Napoleon to arrive back home, not just to find out how badly his campaign went, but to enjoy telling him some more bad news.

'Your excellency, or is it your highness?' he said, with a wide grin on his smug face. 'I trust your mission went well?' He could see by the number of hungry soldiers with no boots that it had not.

'I don't want to talk about it,' said Louis-Napoleon. 'Please leave me alone.'

'I am sorry, but I cannot. There has been a bit of trouble while you were away.'

'What kind of trouble?' asked Louis-Napoleon, wondering if perhaps the Luxembourgers had tried to invade them. That he could deal with.

'A miner rebellion at a place called Eureka.'

'A minor rebellion?' he asked. 'It can wait.'

***

One thing history teaches us is that if you are going to take all your available troops and march to invade a neighbouring colony – make sure there are no troubles at home that you might need to leave a few troops behind for. And Louis-Napoleon was clearly not as good a student of history as you are – because he completely forgot about the growing troubles on the goldfields over the issue of taxing the miners. He also never thought anything could get so far out of control that it might need extra troops on hand to manage.

In real life the Eureka Stockade Rebellion was put down by troops, but in our What If history all those troops were up near the Border River, and things played out very differently indeed.

But first let's put on our Really Truly Historically Factual hat and look at what really happened.

The cause of Eureka Stockade Rebellion

The city of Ballarat was known at the time as Ballaarat – reputedly coming from two First Nations words "Balla" and "Arat", that meant resting place. And it was home to one of the largest goldfields in Australia in the 1850s.

It had attracted over 30,000 people to the goldfields– and about one-third of them were Irish, who had brought with them a strong sense of liberty and justice and all those things that Irish people lamented they were denied by the English in Ireland. There were also people from other nations who had fought for liberty, including North Americans.

The first pubs had just been allowed to be built on the goldfields, and one of the most popular was the Eureka Hotel. Unfortunately, the owner of the pub, James Bentley, was a lot less popular.

Also, the newest governor of the new colony of Victoria, Sir Charles Hotham, was a man who liked to count the pennies. Not only did he wind back on government spending, but he determined that the miners could afford to pay more in licence fees. He authorised more frequent inspections of licences on the goldfields, and those who could not produce them were arrested.

That also made him very unpopular.

Tensions were high when two unfortunate events happened that triggered things to explode.

Firstly, James Scobie, a young Scots miner broke into the Eureka Hotel after closing hours and demanded a drink. He was not only thrown out, but James Bentley had him beaten to death.

Almost immediately after that, the disabled Armenian servant of Ballarat's Catholic priest was assaulted by police for not having a gold mining licence – despite not being a digger.

In court, he was actually fined for assaulting the police! And then the publican James Scobey was found not guilty.

The miners were outraged! On 17 October 1854, about 5,000 miners gathered outside the Eureka Hotel and first pelted it with rocks, looted it of grog, then burned it to the ground.

In response the police arrested three men for the attack on the hotel. In response to that response 10,000 miners gathered and formed the Ballarat Reform League. Then an even bigger crowd, of about 15,000 people, assembled under a new flag – the Southern Cross – and burned their licences in protest to how they were being treated.

The Eureka Rebellion had begun.

CHAPTER 20

So in both the real and in the What If version of history we have all these angry miners determined to defend their rights, and standing under a new flag of their own making. And for either the British colonial government in real life or the French colonial government in our What If version of history – this was treason! Don't ask me why, but for many people a random bit of cloth with particular patterns on it is very sacred and replacing that random bit of cloth with your own random bit of cloth was a treasonous outrage.

Also burning licences was a challenge to the government's authority. And calling for liberty was just plain annoying. Something had to be done to stop this rebellion!

But in our What If version of history, you will remember that all the French soldiers had gone north in Louis-Napoleon's crazy plan to invade New South Scotland. And that meant there were no soldiers to send to the goldfields.

So when the rebels raised their flag and built their stockade, the police were very worried. There were thousands of angry miners and only a dozen or so of them. And let's give the rebels a few more advantages, with a What If builder who really knew how to make a fort properly, with lots of spiked poles, pointing outwards, and no gaps in the planks for attackers to squeeze through, or even shoot through, and plenty of cover for the rebels to hide behind.

And while there has been a lot of conjecture about there being police spies in amongst the rebels, reporting back to the police what they heard and spreading false rumours, let's presume that the rebel leaders knew who the spies were. And rather than throw them out of the stockade, they fed them false stories that they passed back to the French police. Such as they were expecting several hundred well-armed miners to join them from Le Bendigo. And they were digging a mine shaft under the police camp to blow them all up.

The Attack on the Eureka Stockade

The leaders of the Eureka Rebellion decided to build a stockade to defend themselves. A stockade is the sort of fort you'd build if you didn't have enough wood to make proper walls. It was really a loose collection of barrels and planks and rope.

A lot of history books show it about as strong a fortification as a suburban wooden fence, but it is more likely to have been much less solid.

The rebel's main leader, Peter Lalor, had the Southern Cross flag hoisted in the middle of the stockade and the diggers pledged, "We swear by the Southern Cross to stand truly by each other, and fight to defend our rights and liberties."

Thing were looking good for the rebels, who were supported by about 200 Californians armed with pistols – the closest they had to a fighting unit. But a false rumour that a military unit was marching from Melbourne led to the Americans riding off to intercept them.

There were very few men left at the stockade on the evening of Saturday 2 December. Many had left to either go to the pubs for a drink, or to go back to their tents for a sleep, firm in their belief that the soldiers would not attack them on a Sunday.

But of course the soldiers did just that.

A few days earlier, when the British troops had marched into Ballarat to reinforce the police there, some drunken miners had taken shots at them – hitting and killing their drummer boy. The soldiers were very angry about this and determined to seek revenge over it.

At about 3am on the Sunday morning 282 soldiers and police stormed the small hill the stockade was built on. There were only about 150 men sleeping there that night who were woken up to gunshots and troopers with bayonets attacking them.

The men in the stockade tried to defend themselves, shooting back at the soldiers, but they were heavily outgunned. The defenders chose to surrender, after about 15 minutes of fighting, firm in their belief that the soldiers wouldn't attack people who had surrendered.

But of course the soldiers did just that.

Men and women were shot and stabbed, tents with children in them were set alight, and by the end of the battle 22 diggers and six soldiers had been killed.

One of the diggers, 19-year-old Samuel Lazarus, wrote at the time: "Stretched on the ground in all the horrors of a bloody death lay 18 or 20 lifeless and mutilated bodies ... Newly-made widows recognising the bloody remains of a slaughtered husband – children screaming and crying around a dead father."

The rebel leader Peter Lalor – with his left arm shattered by a soldier's bullet – escaped, but 114 others were taken prisoner.

The Eureka Stockade Rebellion (known at the time as the Eureka Massacre) was over – and while it might have been a failure for the miners, it actually ended up being successful in leading to changes for miner's rights. As such it was a pivotal moment in Australia's democratic history.

So the police got into a bit of a panic, and moved their tents and sleeping location every night, listening for the sound of digging beneath them.

And when they had reported to Melbourne about the diggers flying the Eureka flag and swearing an oath of allegiance to it, this was considered an act of war from within. Louis-Philippe, sitting in charge of things in New New Paris in Louis-Napoleon's absence, decided he had better do something about it.

To his mind this was undoubtedly a secret invasion of the French Colony by the English and Irish. And Americans. And Italians. And Germans. And maybe even the Chinese. This was his chance to prove that he could save the colony. So he gathered up all the guards and police he could find in New New Paris – about 50 or so, and sent them off to Le Ballarat with instructions to put down the rebellion.

Then he went and had a nap in the sun and thought about all the changes he would make when he was made Emperor or King of the colony. He didn't really care which.

But you can guess what happened, right?

Well the police got lost on their way to Le Ballarat and ended up in Le Bendigo. They searched around for any sign of trouble, or a stockade, or rebels with a flag, and not finding anything they turned around and marched back to New New Paris, convinced it had all been a false rumour.

And meanwhile, at Le Ballarat the couriers bringing the orders to attack the rebels and destroy the stockade did not get lost. He gave the unfortunate French police the orders and they decided the only way to succeed without reinforcements was to come up with a sneaky plan.

Similar to real life, the police decided to attack the stockade very, very early on Sunday morning. On the Saturday night they pretended to go to bed, so as not to alert anybody who might be watching them.

Now here's a thing, if you have ever gone to bed planning to wake yourself up quietly after midnight (like maybe you had thought of catching Santa Claus or the Easter Bunny when you were younger) you'll know just how hard it is without an alarm clock of some kind. And the French police didn't want an alarm clock going off and warning people that something was up. They were just as sure they'd wake up as you probably were when you wanted to find out if the whole Santa Claus thing was real or not.

And you can guess what happened.

Of course you can. They slept in.

The head of the police was the first to wake up, with the light starting to ring the hills about them. He rushed around to wake all the other police and they got their guns and boots on and hurried off to the stockade, telling each other there was still time to take the miners by surprise.

But of course there wasn't.

The miners had decided that a well-armed group of men needed to sleep in the stockade every night, and that other sentries needed to keep an eye on the police. So from the very moment the police had gotten dressed and were sneaking along through the miners' tents, one of the sentries fired his pistol into the air as a warning.

Immediately the diggers in the stockade woke up and ran to their posts. The police, in their dark blue uniforms, were easy to see against the dirty white tents they were sneaking past, and as the morning light grew every man in the stockade could see them coming.

The French leader, still convinced they could make the attack work, gathered his men close to him and said, 'Quietly now, we attack!'

Which is a pretty dumb thing to tell anyone, because as soon as you say 'attack!' they will jump to their feet and start running and shouting. I don't know what it is about needing to shout while you run in an attack – but it's a thing. Trust me.

So even the near-sighted diggers who had lost their spectacles were able to know where the French soldiers were by the sound of them.

Peter Lalor, who was in command of the rebels, stood behind a solid wooden barricade and looked at the police running up the hill towards them and shook his head. Were they crazy? Was this attack a distraction to trick them from a real attack somewhere else?

'Shall we shoot them down?' a digger beside him asked.

Now it would have been easy to just say Yes, and for the diggers to shoot the French police as they ran up the hill. But in our What If version of events, Peter Lalor knew how that would play out. The attack would be called a massacre. But a massacre of the police by the rebels. They would forever be looked on as murderous villains, not people fighting for liberty.

So he said, 'No. Let them reach the walls. Then we will disarm them.'

So the French police kept running and yelling and maybe shooting their guns in the air, and perhaps even telling themselves they had a chance of victory as nobody was shooting back at them.

But then they reached the high wooden walls and stopped. They had no way of getting over them. They had not brought ladders or axes or anything.

The French police slowly all stopped shouting and just stood there in confusion. One man emptied his pistol into the wooden planks, but none of the bullets even penetrated the thick wood there.

'Uh – what do we do now?' one of the policemen asked their leader.

'I think you surrender,' cried Peter Lalor from the other side of the fence, and suddenly about 50 or more diggers stood over the fort with their guns pointed at the police.

'Should we attack them?' asked one of the less intelligent policemen.

'I think not this time,' said the leader and put his arms in the air.

The battle was over in less than 15 minutes and news spread around the goldfield quickly. The police had surrendered, and all been taken captive. They were tied up and sitting under the new Eureka flag looking quite miserable. All through the day diggers and their families came to taunt the policemen, getting payback for the way they had been treated in the licence raids.

One woman even took the trousers off several of the police and took them away to make baby clothes out of.

It was worse than being defeated in battle for the police. It was an utter humiliation.

The women of Eureka

A thing about history is that an awful lot of it has been told and written by men (his-story) and we need to remember that there were an awful lot of women involved too, whose stories also need to be told.

For instance, at Ballarat, at least a third of the people there were women – and many women were involved in the protests.

Notable women included Clara du Val who edited the local *Ballarat Times* after her partner Henry Seekamp was arrested. She ran articles supporting the rebels.

Another woman, Sarah Hamner, ran a theatre that was used for protest meetings.

And Elizabeth Wilson who had a shop inside the stockade, was said to have loaded her husband's gun during the battle and then hid one of the rebels under her petticoats, possibly saving him from death.

CHAPTER 20

CHAPTER 21

Breaking a Few Eggs

Louis-Philippe felt just as humiliated as those policemen when he heard the news from the goldfields that the miners had now declared an Independent Territory of the Southern Cross. A place where no man would have to pay taxes to the French, and all leaders would be voted in democratically.

His plan had not gone well, and it made him look like a fool. Even the servants were sniggering at him behind his back. He couldn't dab and he couldn't come up with a good plan. His only saving grace was the news that Louis-Napoleon was returning from the north, having failed to invade New South Scotland (despite him telling everyone it was a great victory). Some of those pesky historians had gotten back to New New Paris first and were telling everyone what really happened.

So the score was a tie - Louis-Philippe 0 vs Louis-Napoleon 0.

Bur Louise-Philippe was cunning and he knew that if he could find a way to dump all the blame onto Louis-

Napoleon he still might come out on top. So he sat out in his nap chair in the sun and tried to come up with a grand idea that would make it Louis-Philippe 0 vs Louis-Napoleon minus 1. Technically a victory.

Louis-Philippe

He decided he need to get Louis-Napoleon to lead his exhausted troops to Le Ballarat where they would be defeated by the well-organised miners.

But you know that is not the way things turned out, right? When Louis-Napoleon heard what had happened, rather than deciding to lead his failed army to Le Ballarat (or the newly Independent Territory of the Southern Cross) he said, 'If you break the eggs, you clean up the kitchen.'

It took Louis-Philippe a little while to understand what this meant. Firstly because he tended to take everything too literal, and looked around him for broken eggs, and secondly because he'd never cleaned a kitchen in his life, having servants to do all those things.

When he finally got it, he asked, 'You want me to go and negotiate with the rebels?'

'Non,' said Louis-Napoleon. 'I want you to go and crush the rebels and return the honour of New New France!'

'Oh…' said Louis-Philippe. Because crushing wasn't really his thing. Unless you were referring to crushing walnuts to eat them – and even then he tended to have servants do that for him.

'I will need the army,' Louis-Philippe said. 'To do the crushing.'

'They are too exhausted. You can only have 500 men,' said Louis-Napoleon. 'That should be more than enough to defeat a bunch the riff-raff rebel miners.'

Louis-Philippe wasn't so sure. But this was his only chance to become King or Emperor of New New France, so he said, 'It will be enough. I will return victorious!'

He half expected Louis-Napoleon to say something like, 'If you do not, then don't return at all.' But he just waved him away and said, 'I'm going to be lying in my bath for a day or two.'

And that's how the second battle for Eureka began!

CHAPTER 22

The Second Battle for Eureka

Now I know there are a few readers who have been turning the pages of this book in the hope of getting a big battle. (I don't want to disappoint you, but there is a good chance you are going to grow up and become like one of those uncles who comes around to visit and only watches war movies and expects a big fat war history book for Christmas each year).

And maybe you were expecting a big battle at the Eureka stockade and were a bit disappointed to get a big surrender instead. And maybe you are thinking of putting this book down right about now, and going to see if any of your uncle's books are written for kids.

Well, the good news is that I don't want to disappoint you anymore. So maybe it's time to get to that battle you've been waiting for. Because one thing the miners in the newly formed Independent Territory of the Southern Cross had figured out was that the French would not take their presence without a fight.

A real fight, right?

But here's a thing about history, while there were lots of battles that did happen – there were also lots and lots that didn't ever happen. The Romans, for example, were very good at paying invading armies to leave them alone. And many large almost-battles in history were settled by diplomacy and agreement rather than going to war.

Battles that never happened

During the US Civil War there was some pressure on the United Kingdom to fight against the North. The British, after all, had lost the colonies there and were still a bit disgruntled about it.

In 1861 American forces actually boarded a British ship to arrest some Southern officers on their way to Britain to try and get more support from them. The British were not impressed with this and wrote a very nasty letter to Abraham Lincoln that could well have tipped them into war.

But Prince Albert – Queen Victoria's husband – although on his death bed dying of typhoid fever, got the letter and amended it so it was not so threatening and insulting, and war was averted.

There were also planned battles or wars between the USA and Canada, with both drawing up plans to invade the other. And the Southern forces in the Civil war had plans to invade Mexico.

They were all wars that never happened.

During the Cuban Missile Crisis in 1962, when the Russians put nuclear missiles in Cuba, in retaliation for the US putting nuclear missiles in Turkey – many people thought it a certainty that the world was going to tip into nuclear war. But it was averted by a bit of diplomacy – with both sides agreeing to take away their missiles and tell their own people that they were victorious.

More recently in 1989 when the Berlin Wall was opened between East and West Berlin in German, it was quite a close thing as to whether the East German border guards were going to let the people cross to the west or stop them with violence. But common sense prevailed, and a shooting battle against civilians was averted.

So now that you know there were a lot of battles in history that never happened, you are probably now thinking that the Second Battle for Eureka was also a battle that didn't happen.

Well almost.

CHAPTER 23

The Almost Second Battle for Eureka

So Louis-Philippe set off for Le Ballarat with several hundred soldiers, after he had spent two hours whooping them up into a state of excitement. You know the normal stuff any government says when they want to turn the public against another group of people: a threat to our way of life, don't speak our language, don't fit in with us, are all criminals, coming to steal your jobs, etc etc etc.

The outraged French troops marched off to teach those terrible miners a lesson. But as we know the miners were expecting them and had a bit of time to think about things. Now they could have stopped mining, and spent their time building stronger defences, preparing for a long and costly battle. And there were a few hot heads who wanted this to happen. But their leaders were clever enough to realise that they were miners, not soldiers, and they had already had one lucky break and it was unrealistic to expect a second one.

So they asked a few key questions, which is always a good thing to do when you are thinking of ways of avoiding a fight. Firstly, what did the miners have that the French did not? The answer to that was easy – gold.

Second question: What did the French have that the miners did not? The answer to that was – no gold.

Peter Lalor, the head of the Eureka Rebels, asked a third very important question: What if we pay the French in gold, not to attack us?

Not all the miners saw sense in this, and many protested that it was their gold, not the French's, and they had been taking too much money in licence fees already.

So Peter Lalor sat down and did a few sums for them on a blackboard. Yeah, just like your teacher might, but you probably don't have a blackboard any more in your classroom – and Peter Lalor sure as heck didn't have a whiteboard.

First, he wrote down how many days they miners would have to be away from their gold mines getting ready for a battle, and then how long it might take fighting the battle, and then he estimated how much time would be needed in the follow up to the battle, like burying dead people and looking after the wounded and so on. About 40 days, he estimated.

Then he made a guess at how much gold they would dig up collectively if they did not go to war and just stayed in their mines.

Then he proposed they offer the French half that much gold.

'You still get to keep half of the gold that you would dig up, and nobody gets injured in a battle,' he said. 'How does that sound to you?'

Now even the angriest miners stopped and thought hard about that. Because no matter how angry they were, and how much they wanted to defeat the French, and how much they didn't want to hand over any of their gold – the numbers on the blackboard were pretty sensible.

Peter Lalor could see some of the slowest miners adding up the sums on their fingers.

It made too much sense not to agree too.

So when Louis-Philippe and his army finally came into sight, the rebels sent a small delegation out with a white flag.

Louis-Philippe was delighted of course, as he believed it meant the miners were so afraid of him that they were going to surrender, and he would go back to New New Paris a hero. Louis-Philippe, plus 1 vs Louis-Napoleon minus 1!

He was a bit disappointed to hear that the miners wanted to propose a peace settlement. A part of him wanted battle, so that he could prove he was better than Louis-Napoleon, but a part of him displayed some common sense too and he also did the sums.

I know I said that whenever gold is involved people lose all common sense and go a bit crazy – but in this case Louis-Philippe actually became so crazy that he saw common sense. Trust me, it's a thing.

But he told the miners, 'I agree to this, but on one very big condition!'

The miners heard what he had to say, were very surprised by it, but said they'd go back to their members and discuss it. It was quite a difficult discussion as many miners didn't want to accept the condition, but in the end they decided it was probably for the best.

CHAPTER 23

And that is how Louis-Philippe became the first Governor of the Independent Territory of the Southern Cross. Just a figurehead, with no real powers, but the Governor nevertheless. Of course, he had to spend quite a bit of time talking to his soldiers about what great fellows the miners actually were, and how they would contribute greatly to the colony and would help New France prosper and might learn French one day with their help and would do all the dirty jobs around the new colony etc etc etc. The same things any government says when they want people to forget the last message they had told them about different people, and now want them to be accepted.

Peter Lalor

Peter Lalor was born into a rebellious family in Ireland who were very active in fights for Irish freedom. He came to Australia in 1852 and arrived at the Eureka diggings at Ballarat in 1854.

He became leader of the movement almost by accident, being the only key organiser there at Bakery Hill when the new Southern Cross flag was raised.

He was wounded in the left arm during the battle of the Eureka Stockade and was hidden from the troopers by supporters. He was later smuggled out of town and his arm was amputated at the shoulder. When those who were arrested at the rebellion were acquitted by a sympathetic jury, the arrest warrant against him was withdrawn.

He then stood for the new Victorian Parliament and was elected. Though as time passed he became less radical and more conservative. He ended up supporting Chinese workers being brought in to break a miners' strike, he opposed the universal right to vote, and he even supported laws that favoured the rich over the poor.

Raffaello Carboni

Raffaello Carboni was a highly-educated Italian miner who wrote one of the first books on the events of the Eureka rebellion. In Italy he was a strong supporter of Italian nationalism and had fought for that cause.

He arrived in Australia in 1853 and became a member of the miners central committee at Ballarat. He spoke out for miners of all backgrounds when at the rebellion he called on miners "irrespective of nationality, religion or colour to salute the Southern Cross as a refuge of all the oppressed from all countries on Earth".

He was one of the 13 men arrested after the battle for the Eureka Stockade and was tried for treason, being portrayed as a foreign troublemaker. He was acquitted with the others in March 1855.

He was later elected to the local court in Ballarat and adjudicated mining disputes. His book, *The Eureka Stockade*, was published in 1855 and is the only full first-hand account of the uprising.

He stated that one of the key reasons he wrote it was so that his brave comrades who had died at the battle would be remembered: "...it is in my power to drag your names from an ignoble oblivion, and vindicate the unrewarded bravery of ... yourselves!"

Rafael Carboni later went back to Italy where he died at the age of 57.

CHAPTER 24

Meanwhile, in New New Scotland

Let's now have a check in on what has been happening in all the other colonies while the Eureka Rebellion was going on. Of course, they were all following the events with the greatest of interest. They were half hoping that the Independent Territory of the South Cross would succeed and diminish the power of the French, and they were half hoping it would fail because it might set a bad example for similar independence movements within their own colonies.

In New South Scotland the Governor has called a meeting with his top aides to discuss the situation.

The military aide has been trying to find a way to take credit for the Eureka Rebellion and the creation of the Independent Territory of the Southern Cross. He has also been trying to convince everyone that it was his plan all along that they didn't actually invade New New France, but just drew the French army away so they could not stop the rebellion.

But as silly as most of the aides are, none of them are actually that silly.

'So you are saying that the invasion of New New France was not an abject military failure?' asks the administrative aide.

'Well in military terms you often allow a tactical failure for a strategic victory,' he says.

'So you are admitting it was a military failure,' says the administrative aide.

'Yes, but only to allow a grander victory.'

'I really don't like the word failure,' says the Governor – who doesn't really understand the difference the military aide is arguing between strategy and tactics. They are all the same to him (and to most people, to be honest).

'A backwards advance, perhaps?' says the top aide, who is today demonstrating her multi-tasking skills by making an embroidery of a landscape while she attends the meeting. 'So when there is a drought and the crops don't grow we don't need to consider it a failure to get a harvest – it is just the crops are having a backward advance. And it somehow contributes to a strategic victory somewhere else that we had nothing to do with, yes? That will make the hungry farmers feel better, I'm sure.'

The military aide feels he is losing the argument and starts to sulk a little lower in his chair.

The Governor raps his knuckles on the desk before him to bring a bit of order and says, 'I think we might just put that unfortunate military incident behind us, and not mention it in any dispatches we write to London.'

He gives everyone his best stern Governor look and they all nod their heads in agreement. 'Good,' he says. 'Now let's get back to the key matter about getting some of that gold in New New France. Tell me, this newly Independent Territory of the Southern Cross – they'd be willing to share their gold with us, wouldn't they? I mean, most of the citizens are British, yes?'

'Well,' says the top aide. 'According to our spies, they are mostly Irish, with a lot of Americans and other Europeans – and they don't actually feel much like sharing with us. Too many years of bad relations with the British I gather.'

'What?' asks the Governor. 'That's most unsporting of them. After all the things the British have done for them over the years.'

'Which things would they be exactly?' asks the top aide. 'Would that be years of oppression in Ireland and buying all the country's corn during the potato famine. And would that be high taxes of the American colonies and going to war to stop them becoming independent, and then following that up with trade wars with them and many of the other countries of Europe?'

The Governor looks at his other aides, hoping one of them will be outraged and speak up on his side, but they are all looking at the floor and the ceiling and the bookcases. Because she is basically right. The citizens of the Independent Territory of the South Cross have no real reason to be supportive of the British endeavours to get their gold.

This time it is the Governor who sits a little lower in his chair and sulks. 'Very unsporting of them,' he grumbles.

CHAPTER 25

Having a Tough Talk About Finances

And down in New New France, Louis-Napoleon has gathered his top aides and is complaining about the treachery of Louis-Philippe.

'How dare he set himself up as head of this so-called Independent Territory of the Double Cross,' he says. 'How ungrateful! After all I did for him.'

His aides look at each other, unable to think of anything significant that their Emperor – or maybe it is King today – actually did for Louis-Philippe. He never gave him his own lands like he asked. He never let him share power in any way. He never even let him hang one of his portraits in the palace.

And maybe palace is a bit of an exaggeration for the building the King – or Emperor – lives in. It is a nice building, of course, and by colonial standards it is very grand – but why he insisted on calling it a palace is unclear. After all, it leaks when it rains and is very cold in winter and very hot in summer.

'Are you listening to me?' Louis-Napoleon demands, seeing the looks on the faces of the men about him.

'Of course, sire,' his top administrative aide says. 'What could be more important than listening to you?'

'Perhaps the state of our finances,' says the financial advisor softly.

'What?' asks Louis-Napoleon. 'What are you suggesting? That we are in financial trouble?'

'Well, frankly yes,' says the financial advisor.

'But we are a rich colony,' Louis-Napoleon says. 'We have all this gold.'

'Had all this gold,' says the financial advisor. 'I think you'll find that the Independent Territory of the Southern Cross has most of the gold now.'

'Double Cross!' Louis-Napoleon corrects him.

'Of course.'

'And what about our gold reserves?' Louis-Napoleon asks. 'Last I checked we had plenty of gold reserves.'

Your Financial Wealth
Balance: 0.00

'Yes, had is the key word. It is very expensive to send an army off to war. Particularly when it comes back again without a victory.'

The military advisor sits a little lower in his seat and sulks.

'What are you saying?' demands Louis-Napoleon.

'We are broke.'

'Tell me plainly,' Louis-Napoleon says. 'I can take it.'

'We are broke,' the financial aide repeats.

'Tell me in plain French that does not sugar-coat the situation,' Louis-Napoleon says.

'We are broke,' says the financial aide a third time.

'Are you implying that we are broke?' says Louis-Napoleon in horror.

The financial aide pinches the top of his nose between his thumb and forefinger, like he can feel a headache coming on. 'That is what I am implying,' he says.

'Well you should come out and say it,' says Louis-Napoleon angrily.

'Yes, forgive me,' says the financial aide. 'I will speak more plainly next time.' He looks at the other aides for support and they roll their eyes like they have all had these types of conversations with Louis-Napoleon before.

'So what do you recommend?' Louis-Napoleon asks the men around him.

'Well,' says the financial aide. 'There are really only two ways to fix finances. We need to spend less and earn more.'

'Spend less?' asks Louis-Napoleon, like he does not understand the words.

The financial aide looks at the other aides for support. But they look at him dumbly. They are not the type of people who really understand the concept of spending less either. Like you can say the words to them, but they just don't quite understand what those words mean.

'Just tell me in plain words,' says Louis-Napoleon. 'I can take it.'

The financial aide sighs and pinches the top of his nose again.

CHAPTER 26

El Gladstono

Meanwhile way up north in Nuevo Nuevo Spain the Governor has also called a meeting of his aides. He is feeling rather pleased. He has heard a report that gold has been discovered half-way up the coast of the colony.

'Tell me about the gold,' he says to his aides, his eyes gleaming like a conquistador about to raid an Incan temple.

'Well,' says his financial aide, examining his notes. 'It appears that a fellow named Senor Chapple discovered traces of gold at a small settlement called El Gladstono.'

'That is splendid,' the Governor says. 'We shall finally be as rich as New South Scotland and New New France.' He punches the air.

'Um, perhaps not,' says his financial aide.

The Governor looks at him and scowls. 'Why not?' he asks.

'Well according to our reports, 15,000 miners flocked to the area in anticipation of getting rich, but they found that there wasn't actually that much gold there at all, and it was all quickly mined out.'

'That is outrageous,' says the Governor. 'I want to talk to this Senor Chapple. He will have to answer to me.'

'It appears he has gone into hiding,' says the financial aide. 'Evidentially all the miners in El Gladstono want to talk to him as well, and want him to answer to them first.'

'I hope they string him up without his pants on,' says the Governor. 'What a rogue.'

'There is more,' says the financial adviser.

'Yes?' ask the Governor, not liking the way he had said that.

'Most of the miners are stranded with no money and are asking you for support to get back to their homes.'

'Asking me?' asks the Governor. 'No, no, no. They should be asking this Senor Chapple.'

'Who is in hiding and can't be found.'

'Then they should be asking Spain, or maybe their parents, or putting out a crowd-funding request in the newspapers or...'

The aides wait for him to run out of ideas.

'And what will happen if we refuse to aide them?' the Governor asks. 'I mean if they were stupid enough to lose all common sense and go chasing for gold on a rumour?'

'We have heard they are considering copying events in New New France and setting up an independent territory in our colony,' says the military advisor.

'Oh!' says the Governor. He knows his masters in Spain will not be happy that the gold rush in El Gladstono has not proven to be profitable. But he also knows they will be much more unhappy if an independent territory is set up in the middle of the colony. They would probably recall him to Spain and give him a job like being in charge of all the public toilets at the bullfights across the country.

'All right then,' sighs the Governor. 'Let's see what we can do to help them get back home. And somebody, anybody, come up with a plan to get us some of the other colonies' gold!'

CHAPTER 27

Gold, Guano and Grapes

And over in New New Holland they were having troubles of their own. The Governor, a very tall thin man with an appetite for grapes, was being told yet again of his colony's continued failure to finding gold.

'We have sent men out in all directions,' his aides say. 'And they have continued to find more valuable metals such as iron and copper and tin and ...'

'But it is not gold!' says the Governor, smacking his hand on the table. 'The French have gold, the British have gold, the Spanish have gold, why not us? We have the biggest territory. We must have gold somewhere. People are just not looking hard enough.'

'Well,' says his financial adviser, 'I was going to suggest we join the Luxembourgers in mining guano. It is very profitable.'

The Governor had finally sent someone to the Luxembourgian territory who was not a relative of his wife, and they had come back and explained all about the Guano and how valuable it was. Every bit as valuable as gold.

The Governor had then finally realised the box of bird poo was not meant to be an insult, called off plans to invade the Luxembourgian territories, and sent a short note of thanks to the Luxembourg Governor. Well, he didn't actually send the note of thanks – one of his aides did it for him. The same aide it should be added, who had taken the guano home and was using it to grow very large and healthy vegetables in his backyard garden.

'No, no, no,' says the Governor. 'I will not be known as the Governor for Bird Poo! Was the Dutch East Indian Company built on poo? Was the wealth of our country built on poo? No. If it is not gold I am not interested.'

'There is one other possibility,' says an aide softly.

'Is it about gold?'

'Not actually.'

'Then I don't want to know.'

'What about grapes?'

The Governor turns his head and looks at him closely. 'What type of grapes?' This has his interest because all his grapes have to be imported, which is very expensive, and they are often rotten when they arrive.

CHAPTER 27

'Well, I'm not sure what type, but some Germans have approached us with the idea of taking up land to the north of here. They say it is ideal grape growing country.'

'Is it indeed?' asks the Governor.

'So they say. They believe they can establish great vineyards and wineries there. They say it could contribute greatly to the wealth of the colony.'

The Governor thinks about it. 'Agreed. Give them a land grant. But they will need to pay their taxes in grapes.'

'Not in gold?' asks one of the aides.

The Governor looks at him and frowns. 'Can you peel gold and feel the sweet taste of it all around your mouth when you bite into it?' he asks.

The aides look at each other roll their eyes. They wonder if this Governor will still be here by the time the vines have matured enough to grow grapes, and what odd obsession the next Governor might have.

Still, they think, they should be able to sell grapes and wine to the other colonies and finally find a way to get some of their gold.

CHAPTER 28

It All Comes Back to Taxes

And finally we check in on the office of the Governor of the colony of New New Luxemburg. His aides are sitting around him and running through all the profits they have made from selling guano to Europe. They are all feeling very pleased with themselves. In fact they are feeling just a little too pleased with themselves. For while gold is known to make people lose common sense and act idiotic, it turns out that dried bird poo can also make people just as crazy.

'What do our spies tell us about bird poo deposits in the other colonies?' the Governor asks.

His military aide says, 'It is hard to say, since they don't seem to put any value on bird poo – they are all obsessed with gold.'

'Fools,' the Governor says. 'Long after all the gold has been dug up and shipped off to England and China and America, we will still be rolling in bird poo.'

'I think you mean rolling in the wealth of bird poo, yes?' says another advisor.

'Of course, of course,' says the Governor. But his aides do wonder why he has had a bathtub full of bird poo installed in his residence. He tells them it is for scientific research – but they aren't too sure.

'I am positive they have hidden guano deposits that they aren't telling us about,' he tells his aides.

'Well, it is possible,' one of his aides admits. 'They do have offshore islands and they do have seabirds.'

'And birds have to poo,' says the Governor.

No one disagrees with that.

'And if they aren't using that bird poo, then we might as well take it for ourselves.'

'Are you suggesting a trade treaty?' his financial adviser asks him.

'What kind of a treaty would that be?' the Governor asks.

'Well, we would get to mine the guano and we would pay the other colonies for what we mine.'

'That sounds dangerously like a tax!' says the Governor.

'Oh no,' says the financial adviser. 'A tax is when you have to pay some of your earnings, a trade treaty is where you have to pay some of your profits.'

The Governor thinks on that a moment, trying very hard to see the difference. 'It still sounds dangerously like a tax to me,' he says.

'Some taxes cannot be avoided,' his financial adviser says.

The Governor is shocked. This man must come from a lower-class background as he does not realise that the wealthy and the nobles are never expected to pay tax. Benefit from tax, yes. Actually pay tax, never!

'No, no, no, no,' says the Governor. 'That is completely unacceptable. We need to find another way to get that guano without paying for it. I mean, if the other colonies want to buy it from us like the Governor of New New Holland did, then that's fine. But we are not going to pay them in any way. How do you expect to get wealthy if you pay for the things you get?'

None of his aides had an answer to that of course. But then again, none of them had ancestors who were board members of the Dutch East Indies Company, like the Governor had. And he believed that alone meant he knew how to make lots and lots of money very quickly.

But those of us who remember reading about the Company will know they were also very good at losing all that money very quickly.

CHAPTER 29

Time to Talk About Bushrangers

Now it's time to talk about bushrangers. We can leave most of the Governors of the colonies for a little bit, as they busily scheme and plan and try more and more crazy ways to get the wealth of the other colonies.

Putting on our Really Truly Historically Factual hat once more, the earliest bushrangers in Australia were convicts who had taken to the bush and decided a life of crime was preferable to a life in chains. This was particularly so in Van Diemen's Land where many notable bushrangers emerged, including Martin Cash, Matthew Brady and Michael Howe.

But by the time gold had been found the types of bushrangers that were taking up the trade were quite different. Many of them were either born in the colonies, or had come as diggers and didn't necessarily come from a criminal background. They just decided that a life a crime was preferable to a life of hard toil – and being harassed by the police for being a bushranger was not that different to being harassed by the police for being a miner at the time.

Bushrangers were often viewed by the poor settlers who lived in the bush as either gentlemen bushrangers who were polite and kind, or brave lads being unfairly victimised by the police. As such they became popular folk heroes with poems and songs written about them. The poorer settlers were also willing to help them, providing hideouts and letting them know when the police were on their trail.

Anybody who robbed from the rich was okay in their books. Until they got robbed themselves – then they were crying out for the police to catch those lawless rogues!

The golden age of bushranging ran from about 1850 to 1880 – and bushrangers generally ranged for about two or three years being captured, shot, jailed or hanged.

But this is a What If version of history, right, so we can play a little with timelines and dates to suit our purposes. And for that we need to return to the office of the Governor of New South Scotland, where he has finally been convinced to consider his military aide's plan to send bushrangers to New New France to rob them of their gold. And that includes any gold dug up in the Independent Territory of the Southern Cross.

The military aide has made sure that the Governor's top aide is not at the meeting, to ask him any of the difficult questions she so often asks, and he has a folder of papers with him, with details of different bushrangers.

'So let me get this straight,' the Governor says. 'We will pay these – these rogues – to go to New New France and rob every stagecoach and bank they can, and they will bring the gold back to us?'

'That's basically it,' said the military aide. 'But I think we don't need to actually pay them. We could offer them a percentage of all the gold they steal, for instance.'

The Governor wishes his top aide was at the meeting, as he has a nagging feeling that there is something wrong with this bold plan – but he just can't put his finger on it.

'And can we trust them to do that?' he asks the military aide.

‘I think so,’ he says. ‘The other alternative for them is that we hunt them down and imprison them and hang them.’

‘I see,’ says the Governor. ‘but won’t the French and the military of the Independent Territory of the Southern Cross be hunting them down too? I mean they will want to catch them and imprison them and hang them, won’t they?’

‘Ah yes,’ says the military advisor, ‘but that’s the beauty of my plan, see. When they find things are getting too hot for them, they will just need to cross back over the Border River and be safe.’

‘So you’re saying that our police will no longer be hunting them down?’

‘Well, as long as they bring back enough gold. I think that’s a fair deal, after all. I mean after a couple of years of bushranging I’m sure the average rogue really wants nothing more than to settle down and run a quiet pub somewhere.’

‘Is that so?’

‘I imagine it is.’

‘Well then,’ says the Governor. ‘Let’s look at the applicants.’

The military aide lays the first piece of paper on the desk between them. ‘I think this one is very promising,’ he says. 'His name is Frank Gardiner – though that's not his real name. He is actually Frank Christie.'

'Why do they all have made-up names?'

'Just wait until we get to some of the real creative ones.'

'He's an Irishman I suppose?'

'Scottish actually. Now he's a good candidate because he spent time in New New France, and was arrested for stealing horses there. But he showed great initiative and escaped from a work gang and made his way to our colony. He was again arrested here for trying to sell stolen horses at Yass.'

'But we want a gold thief, not a horse thief!' says the Governor.

'Let me get to that bit. It's quite impressive. So he was released early and put together a gang. He was quite popular with both men and women it appears. And he was able to read – quite astounding – and it is said he carried a pistol in one pocket and a copy of Lord Byron's poems in his other. The gang was a bit of a dream team – some of the best bushrangers operating at the time, including Johnny Gilbert and Dan Charters and Ben Hall. And Frank Gardiner, or Frank Christie or Frank Clarke, demonstrated his ability both to lead men and to plan with military precision.'

'I'm liking the sound of this fellow,' says the Governor.

CHAPTER 29

Description: Frank Gardiner
Age
Build
Eyes
Hair
Marks
Dress
Offence
Date
Sentence

'Yes, with his gang they robbed the Forbes to Orange gold coach at a place called Eugowra Rocks. A very spectacular robbery too, by all accounts. The men all dressed in red shirts with red scarves covering their faces and they attacked in two lines of four, with admirable military precision. Two of the police were wounded and at the sound of gunfire the horses bolted, and the coach turned over, making things very easy for them. They netted £14,000 pounds in gold and bank notes, and used the carriage horses to escape on!'

The Governor splutters. 'What! That's criminal! I mean – that's magnificent. Exactly what we want. I think you should bring the man in for an interview.'

'Well that's the difficult part,' says the military aide. 'After the robbery the gang split up. We have been fortunate enough to catch most of them, but Frank Gardiner has seemingly disappeared. Rumour has it he has gone to New New Spain with his girlfriend – named Kitty Brown.'

'Well, can't we put a reward out for him?' asks the Governor.

'Um – there is already a reward out for him,' says the military aide.

'Oh – of course. Hmmm. Well, put that piece of paper to the side and we'll see if we can't locate him somehow. Who's next?'

CHAPTER 29

The military aide lays down the next sheet of paper.

'Next is Ben Hall.'

'He was one of Frank Gardiner's gang, yes?'

'Yes. You might have heard the songs they sing about him about town too.'

'No.'

'Oh. Well, it doesn't matter. Anyway, he was notable for not changing his name into anything fancy.'

'Peculiar,' says the Governor.

'Well, most of his life was quite normal, until he developed an extreme hatred of police.'

'Why was that?'

'Let me explain. Ben was born in New South Scotland, to convict parents. He worked as a stockman and at the age of 19 married and had a young child named Henry. Things were going well it seems, but his wife left him while he was away working and moved in with another man. A former policeman.'

'Oh dear.'

'That tipped him into joining Frank Gardiner's gang.'

The Governor nods his head. 'I see.'

Description: Ben Hall
Age
Build
Eyes
Hair
Marks
Dress
Offence
Date
Sentence

Hall was arrested for a robbery, but the charge was dismissed in court as it could not be proved he was one of the gang. However, he was definitely one of the men who robbed the Forbes to Orange gold coach – though again they couldn't prove it. But the local police inspector Frederick Pottinger burned down Hall's farm and killed his cattle, just to make a point.'

'Pottinger!' says the Governor and shakes his head. 'I thought sending him out west might disguise his incompetence.'

'Evidentially not,' says the military aide. 'As a result, Hall proclaimed a hatred of all police, put together a gang and started a string of robberies all around the district. It says here he robbed ten mail coaches, held up 21 towns or stations, and stole over 20 racehorses – making him very difficult to catch. Once his gang even bailed up a hotel in Canowindra and treated everyone there to a three-day party of drinking and eating. They even paid all the bills they ran up.'

The Governor raises his eyebrows. 'So the people love him?'

'Of course. And the fact he has never shot a policeman, which is quite extraordinary. Though members of his gang have. Over one hundred robberies have been attributed to him.'

'He sounds like our man then,' says the Governor. 'Send out word to offer him an amnesty to discuss our offer.'

'Splendid,' says the military aide.

Just then there is a knock on the door and a policeman pokes his head in. 'Excuse me,' he says. 'Urgent note.' He steps in and passes it to the military aide, who reads it and says, 'Oh dear.'

'What is it?' asks the Governor.

'Ben Hall. He's just been shot dead. Captured by troopers and riddled with bullets.'

'Damn,' says the Governor. 'Oh well, who's next?'

'This is where they start getting into the exotic names,' says the military aide. 'The first one is Captain Thunderbolt, though his actual name was Frederick Wordsworth Hall. He was also the son of convicts and also started out as a station hand and then turned to stealing horses. He was arrested for this and sent to Cockatoo island but escaped.'

'Good,' says the Governor. 'Shows initiative.'

'He took up with a local woman – you know what I mean – and they ranged all over the north of the colony, sometimes with a gang, sometimes not, and often with younger men who would follow his orders. Police have been trying to catch him for a long, long time, but by all accounts the woman has extraordinary bush skills and helps him escape repeatedly.'

'Sounds very promising,' says the Governor. 'Definitely a contender. Do you think we could contact him?'

'Well, that could be difficult. He has proven very difficult for our men to locate.'

'Tell them to double their efforts. And for heaven's sake, don't shoot him dead when they capture him. Who's next?'

'Another Captain. This one is Captain Midnight.'

'Why are they always Captains?'

The military aide shrugs his shoulders, 'Probably sounds a lot more commanding that Lieutenant Midnight – or it just might be that his own name – Thomas Smith – didn't evoke enough awe or fear in anyone.'

'Alright. Tell me about him.'

'The Captain started out as a cattle thief, blah blah blah, same old story, arrested and when released went back to crime. Blah blah blah, shot a policeman and stole his horse, blah blah blah. Oh. Sorry, he shouldn't be in the pile of applicants.'

'Let me guess,' says the Governor. 'Shot dead by the police.'

'Yes. They shot his horse out from underneath him and then shot him. He died shortly after of his wounds.'

The Governor sighs. 'Who is next?'

The military aide holds up the next piece of paper, reads it and pulls a face. 'No, on second thoughts, not this one.'

'Why not?' ask the Governor.

'He's a bit – um – erratic.'

'Show me,' says the Governor, holding out his hand for the paper. He takes it and reads it over slowly. 'Oh dear,' he says. 'What type of a name is Mad Dog Morgan?'

'One can only imagine where he got such a name,' says the aide.

'So let's see, born John Owen, but also known as John Fuller, also known as John Smith. Convicted and jailed for six years, and then became known as Down-the-River-Jack.' He looks at the aide and says, 'Well I suppose that is better than Captain Down-the-River-Jack!'

'Indeed,' says the aide and then points at the page. 'He was also known as Sydney Bill, Warrigal, Dan the Breaker, Beardie and Jack Morgan. And you'll see the chap has an absolute hatred of authority and has been described by those who he has robbed or attacked as sadistic and murderous and the most blood-thirsty ruffian that ever took to the bush. He has shot policemen and tied men up to trees without their clothing, setting fire to the trees.'

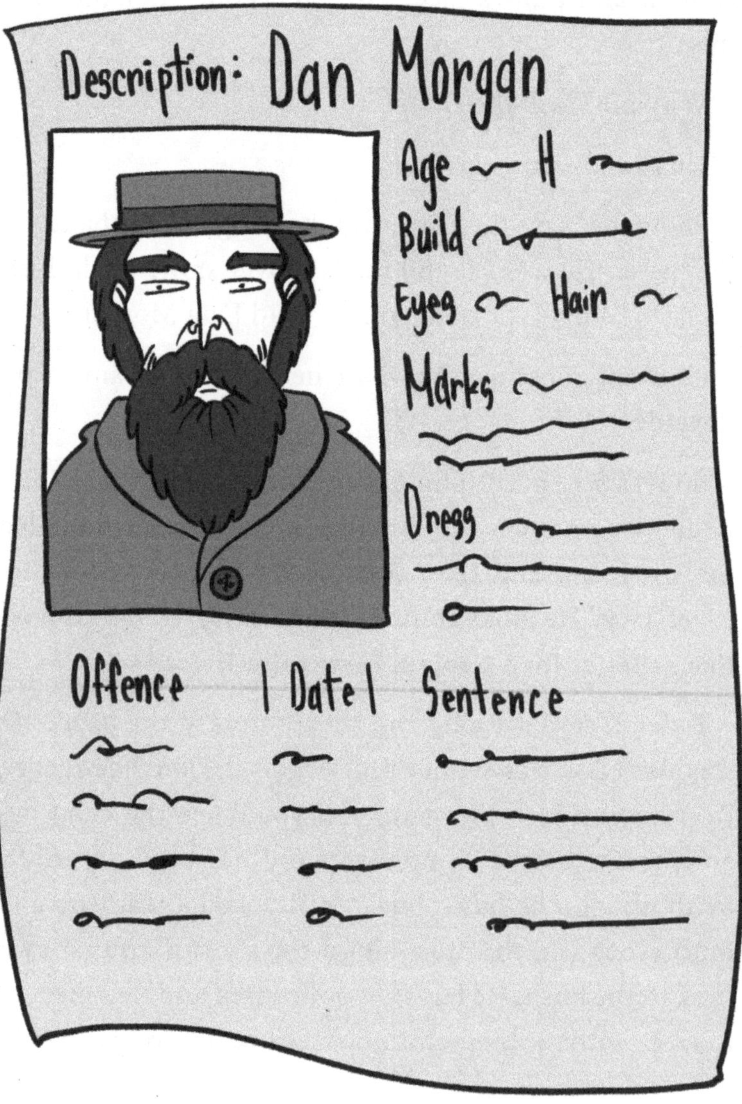
Description: Dan Morgan
Age
Build
Eyes
Hair
Marks
Dress
Offence
Date
Sentence

'Yes, I see,' says the Governor. 'And this is his charge sheet?' He runs his eye down the long, long list of violent crimes, including robbing station after station and shooting a policeman in the face at point blank range. He looks at the military aide and says, 'Yes. Perhaps you're right. I don't really fancy having an interview with the chap.'

That piece of paper is put aside and then the military aide picks up the next one and says, 'This is a long shot, but it could be something the French won't expect.'

'Why is that?'

'He's Chinese.'

'What? A Chinese bushranger.'

'Yes,' says the military aide and places the sheet of paper on the desk. 'He goes by the name of Sam Poo.'

'Poo?' asks the Governor. 'That's not a joke is it, to make me say, you know, I want Poo?'

'No,' says the military aide. 'Though it is believed his real name was Li Hang Chiak and he went by the name Cranky Sam.'

'That's not very imaginative,' says the Governor.

'No, but it was very accurate,' says the military aide. 'By all accounts he was perpetually cranky and would attack either Chinese or Europeans and fly off the handle at any provocation. He shot and killed a policeman who was hunting him. He is also said to be very skilled at living alone in the bush.'

'Ha. I like the idea of the French looking for a Chinaman amongst all the Chinamen in New New France. They won't be able to tell one from the other.'

'Surely that's just a racial stereotype,' says the military aide.

'Of course,' says the Governor. 'Forgive me. But I think this Poo fellow could be very promising. He'd raise a stink in New New France, yes?'

'Things could come to a sticky end,' says the military aide.

Both men laugh so much at their own jokes that they have to wipe the tears from their eyes.

'There is just one problem,' says the military aide finally.

'He's not been shot dead too, has he?' asks the Governor.

'Not quite. But he has been shot in one leg and he cannot ride a horse. We estimate it would take him about six months to walk to the goldfields in New New France with a limp.'

The Governor slumps in his seat. 'Well nobody wants to wait six months for this Poo to arrive.'

The military aide isn't sure if that was a joke or not and watches the Governor for signs of him smiling or laughing. Nothing. So he hides his own smile and says, 'Yes, that is far too long to wait for a Poo.'

Bridget Hall

The Walsh Sisters

The two Wash sisters, Kitty and Bridget, played a key part in the lives of two Australian bushrangers – Ben Hall and Frank Gardiner.

Kitty Walsh had married a man named John Brown in 1858, but left him for Frank Gardiner, and the two of them fled to Queensland after the large gold robbery in 1862. They ran a pub and store at Apis Creek near Rockhampton, where nobody knew who they were.

However, Kitty inadvertently tipped off the police as to where she and Frank Gardiner were hiding when she wrote a letter to her sister Bridget – who had formerly been married to Ben Hall. Bridget's new partner, James Taylor, read the letter and was boasting he knew the whereabouts of Frank Gardiner – which came to the attention of the police.

In 1864 the police went up to Queensland, located and arrested Frank Gardiner. The following year Ben Hall was shot by police.

Kitty tried hard to have Frank freed, but in 1867 she moved in with Richard Taylor – the brother of James Taylor – and then moved to New Zealand.

Maryann Bugg

Maryann Bugg is often said to be Australia's only female bushranger – which is not accurate – though certainly she is one of the very few female First Nations bushrangers.

She was born to a convict and his Worimi wife on the mid-north coast of New South Wales and was moved from place to place as she grew, even spending time at school in Sydney. She married Edmund Baker at the age of 14, but left him some time later.

She met Frederick Ward – Captain Thunderbolt – in 1860, and after his arrest and escape from Cockatoo Island prison they went on a crime spree. Calling herself the Captain's Lady, she often dressed and rode like a man, taking part in several robberies with his gang. Her knowledge of the bush and bushcraft helped them evade the police many times.

She is also said to have taught Ward to read and nursed him back to health when he was shot.

Another account says she was arrested while pregnant, but faked birth contractions and then escaped when the police left her alone to give birth.

She is believed to have had three children to Frederick Ward before his death in 1870, and had 15 children over her life, spending her last years working as a nurse in Mudgee, NSW.

There are many monuments to Captain Thunderbolt across areas of New South Wales, but like many women in history, her story is not as well acknowledged.

CHAPTER 30

Tracking the Bushrangers

It is easy to get interested in the exciting life of bushrangers, but we should also spare a thought for the dedicated police who tracked them down. It is also easy to portray police at the time as incompetent and bullying – and this was true for some of them – but there were also hard-working and dedicated policemen.

Also, in any history of bushrangers, we should also be aware of the First Nations people who worked with the police as trackers. Using their bush skills they were excellent trackers and were responsible for catching many bushrangers.

Ben Hall's story, for instance, should always include the story of Bill Dargin who tracked him down. When he had been shot and wounded, he was said to have said to him, "Shoot me dead Billy! Don't let the traps take me alive."

CHAPTER 30

The infamous Clarke Brothers who were bushrangers around Canberra (before the first politicians moved in), were hunted down by a Wiradjuri tracker known grandly as Sir Watkin Wynne. And even Ned Kelly was tracked by trackers from Queensland that he referred to angrily as those "six little devils".

In fact, the police sergeant in charge of those trackers, Sub-Inspector Stanhope O'Conner, campaigned for his troops to receive a cut of the reward. And although the government of the day promised they would pay it – they never did. Sadly the men were said to have ended up living in internment camps as destitutes (with no money or means to support themselves).

Jimmy Governor

There were several First Nation Bushrangers, but they don't get a lot of coverage in many history books (except great ones like this, of course!). Their reasons for turning outlaw were often different to the stories of European Bushrangers too.

Jimmy Governor and his gang were an example. Jimmy was an accomplished person who could read, was a renowned horse breaker and had even worked as a tracker for the police at times.

Despite his skills he was treated badly by white society – particularly when he married a white girl – Ethel Mary Jane Page, who was 16 at the time. Clearly she saw more potential in Jimmy than others did.

He was working on a farm in West Breelong, north of Dubbo, when an incident occurred that demonstrated the racism of the day. The story goes that his wife had gone to the station house to get their ration of flour, where she worked as an unpaid servant. But she was turned away and abused by the station manger's wife, Mrs Mawbey, for marrying a First Nations man.

When Ethel told Jimmy what had happened he became very angry and went to the station house and demanded their ration of flour. The manager said he would look after it, but nothing happened. Getting more and more angry, Jimmy took his brother Joe along with Ethel and friend Jacky Underwood, to go to the homestead at night with him. They were said to have taken a rifle and an axe with them.

They demanded Mrs Mawbey and the family's schoolteacher, Ellen Kerz, apologise for their treatment of his wife. Instead the two women both abused Jimmy again, stating, "You should be shot for marrying a white woman!"

That was the final insult and Jimmy and the others attacked everyone in the house, leaving a 9-year-old boy to escape and raise the alarm.

Taking his brother Joe, his wife Ethel and their baby, and Jacky, Jimmy escaped into the bush. And of course their knowledge of the land, along with Jimmy's knowledge of police tracking, made it hard for anyone to catch them. So began a reign of terror on homesteads of the area. They committed at least 80 crimes and the reward on their heads grew to £1,000.

He was said to have a list of all the people who had treated him poorly and was seeking his revenge on them.

The hunt for the gang was one of the largest manhunts in Australia's history, with about 2,000 civilians and police taking part.

But with a price on his head and increased numbers of people looking for them, he was soon cornered and shot in the mouth. He escaped, but was finally captured over a week later – severely malnourished from being unable to eat with the mouth wound.

Joe and Jacky were also caught.

Ethel, who was pregnant with her and Jimmy's second child when he was hanged, eventually married again, to a First Nations man from Wreck Bay on the south coast of New South Wales. She had nine more children and is remembered for playing an active role in the community.

CHAPTER 31

Enter Ned Kelly

And down in the colony of New New France they were having bushranger problems of their own – although of an altogether different kind. And this is where Van Diemen's Land comes into the story. (I know everyone reading this book in Tasmania has been reading carefully, waiting to find out what happens there in our What If history). The French decided to use the island in pretty much the same way the British had, and exiled all their worst convicts there.

In an effort to keep the colony of New New France free of crime and troublemakers, every time somebody was convicted of a serious offence – like robbery or of speaking French really, really badly – they were shipped off to Van Diemen's Land. As a result the population there slowly grew and grew and as people ended their sentence they decided it wasn't too bad a place to live if you weren't in prison. It had nice scenery and the First Nations people turned out to be willing to trade when some people decided to treat them well, and the ground looked quite fertile for farming.

So many of them stayed there.

Hurry up and arrest me!

And soon, if you lived in New New France and didn't have a job and found things really hard going, it wasn't a bad idea to become a bushranger, get caught and sent to Van Diemen's Land. Because after your sentence was up you could become a farmer there.

But not all bushrangers in the colony were looking for a free ride to Van Diemen's Land. And here we are talking about one bushranger and his gang in particular, who were causing more trouble for the French than all the other bushrangers put together.

You know who I'm talking about right? Ned Kelly and the Kelly gang!

And here's a key question for all you history students out there – Why do you think Ned Kelly has become so famous when so many other bushrangers operating in the same colony, like Alfred Stallard, Black Douglas or Henry Rouse (who went by the peculiar names Codrington Revingston, Carrington Gessington, or Codrington Leviston. Yeah, I know, what was he thinking?) are less known?

Whether it's the real history or the What If history, the Kellys are icons for bushrangers. They have the gang, they have the police victimising them, they have the support of the locals standing up for them, they have their sharing of loot with locals – and they have the armour!

CHAPTER 31

Ned Kelly

You can imagine all the other bushrangers, like Henry Rouse, kicking themselves for thinking that a memorable name like Codrington Revingston would ensure their fame, when the Kellys come along with a simple name and with their metal helmets!

In fact, while the Kelly gang were ranging around the place in the 1870s, another bushranger known as Captain Moonlite (yes, another Captain!) was getting a lot of publicity, and his shootout with police near Wagga in 1879 was covered by newspapers all over the colonies. It was the biggest story of the day.

Until the Kellys shoot out at Glenrowan the following year. Then poor old Captain Moonlite was all but forgotten.

And let's put on our Really Truly Historically Factual hat and look at a quick overview of the Kelly story.

- 1854 or 1855, Edward Kelly born in Beveridge north of Melbourne.
- 1869, 14-year-old Ned arrested for assaulting a Chinese pig farmer.
- 1870, arrested again for assault and later for riding a stolen horse and fighting with police.
- 1878, he is accused of attacking drunken police officer Constable Alexander Fitzpatrick. The stories of the policeman and the Kelly family differ

greatly as to whether Ned was even there. Ned goes into hiding in the bush.

- 1878, a party of four policemen hunting through the mountains to capture the Kelly gang are ambushed by them. Despite being told to surrender, the police fire back and at the end of the shooting three police are dead. The Kelly gang are declared outlaws with a large price on their heads.
- 1878, the Kelly gang hold up a bank in Euroa.
- 1879, the Kelly gang hold up a bank in Jerilderie, NSW.
- 1880, the gang build armour and Ned plans a major confrontation with police at Glenrowan. The plan is to cut the train tracks and a police train will be wrecked. The plan goes wrong when the police are warned by a local schoolteacher and they surround the Inn where the Kelly gang is holed up. Ned Kelly is wounded and captured, and the other three gang members are killed.
- 1880, Ned Kelly stands trial and is hanged.

But in our What If version of events we are going to change things around a bit.

To set the scene, the northeast New New France, has a large population of Irish settlers, who have come looking for gold, but stayed on as settlers of the land. The French allow this as it gives them more people to tax. But before too long the settlers ask that question that all people have asked throughout history when they find themselves outnumbering the people who want to tax them: Why shouldn't we declare ourselves independent of New New France? And look what happened with the Independent Territory of the Southern Cross! Afterall, all the French offer is corrupt and drunken policemen and taxes.

And the Irish settlers know they can easily recruit their own corrupt and drunken policemen. But what they need is a figure-head to rally around. Somebody who hates the French and is willing to stand up to them. Somebody like perhaps maybe a gang of outlaws dressed in armour.

Now in real life there is some conjecture by historians that the attack on the police at Glenrowan was actually part of a plan to trigger a rebellion of the people in the northeast of Victoria. According to some historians Ned was going to fire skyrockets into the night signalling the rebels to rise up in revolt. But when things went badly at Glenrowan and the police had them surrounded Ned dashed out in the darkness – wounded – and warned the men and women to return home and hide.

Then he went back to face the police alone and was shot and captured.

But What If the police had not been able to send troopers up the northeast because they were busy dealing with troubles between the French and the new Independent Territory of the Southern Cross? Or What if the train had been derailed and all the police had been put out of action? Or What if the Kelly gang decided to stop the train and take all the police captive?

What might have happened then?

Well in our telling, the battle at Glenrowan goes very, very different. One minute the police are sitting on their train, telling each other how they are going to be the one who shoots and captures Ned Kelly, and the next the train is bumping badly and then tumbling onto its side.

The police are thrown about and some are knocked out. The others climb out the broken windows, to try and find what has happened.

And they find themselves surrounded by strange-looking men in metal armour. One or two of the French police still have their guns with them and fire at the men. But with a loud ping the bullets bounce off.

The French police are rattled and don't really understand what is happening. Then they see skyrockets shoot up into the night.

'Qu'est-ce que c'est?' they call to each other. 'What is it?'

It is the start of the rebellion! Before too long they are surrounded by dozens of men with guns pointed at them. And their leader, the tallest of them with the large metal helmet on his head, finally takes it off. They see the bearded face of the man they are chasing – Ned Kelly. And he says, 'Lock them up in the Inn!'

They are his prisoners.

Meanwhile, down in New Paris, Louis-Napoleon is listening to his military aide describe to him how they are going to crush the dissent in the northeast.

'We will capture this so-called Kelly gang, who ruthlessly shot three French policemen, and they will be made an example of.'

'Good,' says the Emperor – or maybe the King – he loses track sometimes himself. 'We could do with a victory.'

‘I expect a telegram any moment telling how victorious our forces have been,’ the military aide tells Louis-Napoleon.

‘I look forward to reading it,’ he says. ‘It has been a long time since I had any good news. This could mean a promotion for you, you know.’

The military aide sits up taller in his seat. He could do with some good news too. He is sure that one more embarrassing failure and he will be spending his days cleaning out the horse stables or the palace toilets.

There is a sudden knock on the door and a junior aide puts his head through.

‘Telegram,’ he says.

‘Splendid,’ says the military aide. ‘Give it here.’ He takes it and rips the envelope open. He scans the words there and his face drops.

Louis-Napoleon sees this and frowns. ‘Not what you expected?’ he asks.

‘Very unexpected,’ he says, and he passes the telegram to Louis-Napoleon. It is not from the north of the colony at all. It is from the Governor of Van Diemen’s Land. It says that the free settlers of the colony have decided it is time to cut their ties from the colony of New New France and become their own colony. It also says, please do not send any more convicts there.

Louis-Napoleon crushes the telegram and throws it into the fire and says, 'Zut! Mince! Bon Sang!' (See box on French swear words).

'We will invade them and take the territory back,' vows Louis-Napoleon. 'We will teach them that we are in command. We will not let this go unpunished!'

But he sees the expression on the military aide's face and knows that they will do none of those things. If they can't muster enough men to defeat the new Independent Territory of the Southern Cross there is no way they can fund an invasion of Van Diemen's Land.

Louis-Napoleon is about to swear some more when there is another knock on the door. A different junior aide puts his head inside and says, 'Telegram.'

The military aide snatches it and rips it open. He reads it and then slumps down in his chair, imagining what he might smell like at the end of the day sweeping horse poo out of the stables.

Louis-Napoleon leans over and picks up the telegram. As he reads it his face drops too. It is from the northeast of the colony.

This Ned Kelly outlaw has dared to send him – the Emperor – or King – a mocking message! It says he has taken their policemen hostage and has declared an independent state in the northeast – called New Ireland,

and he invites the King – or Emperor – to visit them one day and be shown the same hospitality they have shown the police he sent to capture him.

Louis-Napoleon crushes up the telegram and throws it into the fire, saying several French swear words that we can't print here in a kid's book, but we can use cartoon swearing - '*%$#$%@$*&!'

French swear words you won't get into trouble for saying (maybe)

Zut! = Darn!

Mince! = Damn!

Oh la vache! = Holy cow!

Sacrebleu! = My goodness!

Bon Sang! = Good grief!

CHAPTER 32

Nearing the End of the Century

So here we are, nearly at the end of the 19th century and each of the colonies in our What If history are struggling with rapid changes driven by wealth and migration, and are pondering how to best face the future. The turn of the century is within sight, and they have asked themselves, what type of a place do we want to be in the 20th century?

For the newest Governor of New South Scotland the answer is a pretty simple one. He is sitting in his office with his top aides – who he has largely inherited from the previous Governor, and he says, 'I have looked closely at all the reports you have prepared for me, and it seems to me that we can no longer rely on gold for wealth. We will need to diversify if we are to continue thriving as a successful colony.'

His aides are happy to hear that for they have long seen that gold has been running out and that the colony needs a more sustainable way to generate wealth than digging holes in the ground.

'We should open up vast new tracts of land for graziers,' he says. 'And turn to sheep and cattle and horses – and maybe even pigs and chickens.'

His top aide, who herself grew up on a farm and recognises farm-mentality in others, looks at him over the top of her spectacles and says, 'But most of the land has been settled. The previous Governors were very generous in giving allocations to friends and family. And then we have to consider the rights of the First Nations people too.'

The Governor looks at her in surprise. 'First Nations people?' he asks.

'You might be more used to the old-fashioned word "natives"', she says, with a disapproving smile. 'But while they might use that term in Nuevo Nuevo Spain and New New France, we like to think we are bit more enlightened here.'

'Of course,' he says. 'We are eternally more enlightened than the French or Spanish. Which is why I am suggesting that we look at taking some of their land – through negotiation or military force.'

'The last time we tried that with New New France it didn't go too well,' says the top aide, while the military aide looks at his shoes.

‘I wasn’t thinking of New New France,’ he says. ‘I was thinking of Nuevo Nuevo Spain to the north. Spain has had better days and can no longer afford a colony of that size. I hear the beaches there are particularly nice too.’

***

And of course, as you have probably guessed, Louis-Napoleon, who was getting on in years now, is holding a similar meeting in New New Paris.

‘We cannot keep losing land to these new republics or independent territories,’ he says. ‘We must expand, rather than contract.’

‘Well that didn’t work too well for your grandfather when he tried to expand into Russia,’ says his military aide, softly.

‘Who said that?’ the old man asks looking around furiously at his aides.

But none of them will meet his eyes.

‘Expansion!’ he says and smacks a hand on the table. Then he puts it under his armpit and rocks back and forward in pain.

‘But the British are too strong at the moment,’ says his military aide.

'The British?' asked Louis-Napoleon. 'Did my grandfather ever defeat the British? I'm talking about New New Holland. They have so much land over there that they wouldn't even notice if we took a great chunk from them.

***

CHAPTER 32

And in New New Holland, their Governor was lamenting the size of the colony he had to manage, with an ever-diminishing budget from the government in Amsterdam. He has called all his advisors into his office and says, 'Our treasury is near empty. The sale of wine and grapes is going well, but we need a scheme to raise more money. And, please, nobody suggest looking harder for gold. I'm now convinced there isn't any our colony to be found.'

His top financial aide says, 'We ran a bake sale at my daughter's school which was quite successful in raising funds.'

'We had a fete at my son's school,' chimes in another advisor.

'No,' says the Governor sternly. 'We need to think bigger than that. We need a whole new way of thinking about money. A way that becomes a driving force for the government to get easy money.'

'Do you have a suggestion?' the financial aide asks.

'Yes,' he says, and he pulls out a coloured brochure from a drawer in his desk.

'What is it?' ask the aides. The brochure has pictures of smiling families and large houses with their own boats and swimming pools.

'It is called real estate,' says the Governor.

'What does that mean?' asks the financial aide (who is also wondering what unreal estate might then be).

'It means we are going to make a fortune selling off chunks of the colony,' says the Governor

***

And in Nuevo Nuevo Spain the Governor has called a meeting to discuss a possible land expansion into the top of New New Holland. But it is a very hot day and most of the aides have sent a servant to tell him that they are having a lunchtime nap.

'Ah well,' says the Governor and he puts a sign on his own door saying, "Do not disturb" and cuddles up in his own large chair for a siesta. They will get around to discussing it all another day.

***

Finally, in the office of the Governor of the colony of New Luxemburg, his aides are sitting around him and running through all the profits they have made from selling guano to Europe.

The Governor is feeling very pleased with himself, because while eventually you can dig up all the gold that exists, birds just keep on pooping.

'What do our spies tell us about the state of things in the other colonies?' the Governor asks.

His military aide opens up a notepad and runs his finger down some points he has made there. 'They are all on the verge of economic depression,' he says. 'Things are not going well in New New France as they no longer have much income from gold, and the cost of running the King or Emperor's court is quite high. The Spanish are also finding the cost of running their colony very expensive too, and frankly they spend too much time sitting on their beaches.'

He moves his finger down to the next point. 'And New South Scotland is also spending more than it earns, as the British, like the French and Spanish, refuse to tax the rich.'

The Governor and the men sitting around the room tut-tut – even though they are exempt from paying any taxes themselves

'Let me see,' says the military aide. 'Ah yes, also all the new independent territories are busy trying to find their own economic bases, now that gold has run out. So all in all, I'd say all the other colonies are in a bit of trouble at the moment.'

'Good,' says the Governor, rubbing his hands together. 'I think it is time to start drawing up plans to invade all the other colonies!'

But that's also another story...

About the Author:

Craig Cormick is an award-winning author and science communicator, with a special interest in history. He has lived in Iceland and Finland and has travelled to Antarctica four times – though he really prefers the tropics. He has written over 30 books for adults and children, and he enjoys messing with history just about as much as history enjoys messing with him. His writing awards include a Queensland Premier's Literary Award, the ACT Book of the Year Award and a Victorian Community History Award. He has also been shortlisted for many awards including twice for an Aurealis Award and twice for the ACT Writing and Publishing Award.